THE RIGHT HOOK OF DEVIN VELMA

JAKE BURT

SQUARE
FISH

Feiwel and Friends
New York

SQUARE
FISH

An imprint of Macmillan Publishing Group, LLC
120 Broadway, New York, NY 10271
mackids.com

Square Fish and the Square Fish logo are trademarks of Macmillan and
are used by Feiwel and Friends under license from Macmillan.

Our books may be purchased in bulk for promotional, educational, or business use.
Please contact your local bookseller or the Macmillan Corporate and Premium
Sales Department at (800) 221-7945 ext. 5442 or by email
at MacmillanSpecialMarkets@macmillan.com.

Library of Congress Cataloging-in-Publication Data is available.
ISBN 978-1-250-21141-5 (paperback) / ISBN 978-1-250-16861-0 (ebook)

Originally published in the United States by Feiwel and Friends
First Square Fish edition, 2019
Book designed by Sophie Erb
Square Fish logo designed by Filomena Tuosto

1 3 5 7 9 10 8 6 4 2

AR: 4.6 / LEXILE: 690L

For Elizabeth

CHAPTER ONE

NARROWED DOWN

I finally figured out why my best friend Devin punched me in the face.

At first I thought it was because I saved his life, but that wasn't it. For a while, I blamed my freezing, only it wasn't that, either. It wasn't even Twitter, the Velma Curse, that stupid dishwasher, or the Golden State Warriors.

Nope.

It was the Double-Barreled Monkey Bar Backflip of Doom.

CHAPTER TWO

THE DOUBLE-BARRELED MONKEY BAR BACKFLIP OF DOOM

The playground at Bennet C. Riley Intermediary School in Los Angeles didn't have much going for it. The soccer field got so dusty that kids spit brown after a good game. The basketball court did have two hoops, but the rims were bent and hadn't had nets since October. I played every day anyway, and that's where I was when Devin marched up, swiped the ball, and made his announcement.

"Game over!" he proclaimed, hugging the ball in his skinny arms. "I need Addison!"

"Me? For what?" I asked.

Before Devin could say, Gage Morris pointed. "Our ball back for Addi? Seems like a fair trade. Teams might actually be even." He looked up at me. "At least, height-wise."

I blushed, rubbing a hand at the back of my sweaty neck.

"Yeah, give it back, Devin," Emil said. He lunged at the ball and knocked it out of Devin's hands. As soon as it rolled into the pack of kids, they snatched it up and loped off like coyotes, leaving my best friend with his hands out wide. His eyebrows were all crooked above his glasses, and he was blinking a lot. I thought he was going to cry again. He'd been doing that almost every day for the past two weeks. Totally understandable, what with the stuff that had happened to his dad, but the Devin I knew didn't mope. Snagging the ball and demanding attention? That was way more Devin.

"You okay?" I asked. "What do you need me for?"

Devin took a deep breath and rubbed his fingers under his nose. He shot the other guys a mean look and grumbled, but then faced me. I smiled. There in his eyes was that old Devin sparkle.

"Lookout . . . ," he whispered. "And cameraman."

"Huh?"

"You'll see," Devin said, and he reached up to grab me by the collar of my Klay Thompson jersey. "To the climber!"

The climber was one of those old wooden monsters with slides and tire swings and splinters. It sat in a patch of wood chips, chewing up space and daring kids to try playing on

3

it without getting hurt. The slide closest to us was the butt-burner, a wide metal one that baked in the sun all day, just waiting to brand the backside of anyone dumb enough to try it while wearing shorts. When we arrived, Devin tested the butt-burner with his thumb, pressing it along the rail. It was January, but that didn't mean much in L.A.; it was eighty degrees the day before.

Satisfied that it was worth the risk, Devin grabbed both railings, his sneakers squeaking as he shimmied up. I shrugged and climbed after him. My size elevens sounded like thunder as they beat against the metal. When we were at the top, tucked away in a sort-of-hidden corner of the tower, I asked again. "Now can you tell me what this is about?"

"You're gonna record me as I do the Backflip of Doom."

My jaw dropped.

"C'mon, Addi. If I can pull off the DBMBBD, it'll be the perfect way to jump-start my plan!"

Jaw.

Just hanging there.

Kind of loose and wiggly.

"Addi, snap out of it. I need you to keep watch and let me know if Ms. Bazemore is coming."

I scanned the playground. Ms. Bazemore, the recess duty

teacher, was on her usual bench, hunched over a pile of papers. She looked to have a stack of about a hundred in her lap, and her red pen was flying across the pages. She didn't glance up once, not even when a four-square ball rolled over and hit her in the shoe. She just kicked it away and kept grading.

The coast seemed clear enough. Still, I winced.

"If . . . if we're caught, I'll freeze."

I wished I knew why everything seemed to shut down as soon as things got tense. It's not like I wanted to feel trapped or anxious. If I could have pinpointed when it started, well, that might have helped, but I wasn't even sure of that. The Great Goldfish Cracker Disaster of '09? The First-Grade Garbageman Fiasco? Something broken from birth? I supposed it didn't matter. What did was how I felt any time it happened.

It was as if my brain ripped in half.

Sometimes, I could actually hear it, like a piece of paper slowly being torn in two. One part of my brain kept talking, telling my voice to speak, my arms to move, my lungs to breathe. The other half just said, "Nope."

Say something funny!

NOPE.

Say something kind!

NOPE.

SAY SOMETHING!

NOPE.

The longer it went, the angrier the first half of my brain got, until it shut down, too. Then the whole thing was, well . . .

Frozen.

It happened any time I had to talk to people I didn't know. Or when I was in front of crowds. Or if I had to explain myself to an adult. There were so many things that made me freeze that I couldn't count them. Sometimes, even worrying about freezing would make me freeze.

And that worry? It was starting up now.

Devin poked me in the shoulder. "You do your job, and we won't get caught. Besides, even if we do, think of it as an opportunity to practice. Your parents are always saying you need more . . . what is it?"

I shuddered. "Exposure."

"Right! Exposure to stuff so you can get over it. Getting caught isn't *so* bad."

We'd have to agree to disagree on that one. A fresh bead of sweat had already trickled down my back, and it had nothing to do with the basketball game.

"And anyway," Devin continued, "we can vouch for each other. As long as we get our stories straight, we'll be fine. Remember how I talked us out of taking the blame for Gage's last prank? When he switched the signs for the supply closet and the faculty bathroom?"

I almost smiled, but then Devin slipped his phone out of his pocket. He unlocked it, tapped his camera app, and started poking me in the chest with it.

"You're not supposed to have that at school," I whispered. "I'm not taking it."

"Yes, you are."

"And you're not doing the Backflip of Doom."

"Yes, I am."

"Why?"

Devin swallowed, looking nervously at the edge of the climber. I couldn't be sure what he said next, but I think it was something like, "To save my dad."

I was about to ask what that meant, but then I looked, too.

The climber had two sets of monkey bars. One was for the little kids. It ran right alongside the higher set. I thought, like, maybe forty years ago, they were painted in bright colors, but now all that was left were little patches of red and yellow where kids' hands and feet couldn't reach so easily. The biggest of those patches sat on the side rail of the higher set of monkey bars. It looked like North America if you tried to wrap our continent around a Pepsi can. That patch was infamous at Bennet C. Riley, because that's where you sat if you were going for it.

It was 1979, or so the story went. Maddie Prufrock, seventh-grade legend, was a gymnast. Eventually got a college scholarship for it and went to UCLA, or something. Anyway, Maddie climbed up there and sat in that exact spot. After licking the tip of her finger to test the wind, she closed her eyes, tucked her legs up to her chest, put her arms in the air, and fell backward. Without being able to see where she was going, she flipped upside down, dropped a few feet, and managed to grab on to two of the rungs of the lower monkey bars like she was doing a handstand on solid ground. She held that pose for a second, just because she could, both legs together and pointed skyward like the barrels of a shotgun raised in salute. Then she calmly completed the flip, bringing her legs over and down to shoot through the bars beneath her. Bang. Just like that, *and* she stuck the landing. The Double-Barreled Monkey Bar Backflip of Doom was born.

I had never even daydreamed about trying it. I was only

twelve, but nearly six feet tall, and most of that was goofy arms and legs, good for grabbing rebounds above the other kids, terrible at fitting into tiny spaces. I looked back at Devin. At least he had a shot, what with how small he was. Of course, being smaller also meant he had that much farther to fall.

"Take your phone, Devin. If you're gonna be stupid enough to try this, I have to be there to catch you."

He pushed the phone back at me. "No way. It won't count if you catch me. I'm pretty sure that's where the 'of Doom' comes in. If there's a big kid there to spot you, it isn't nearly as doomful. It might not even be pitiful. Or fretful. Nobody talks about the Double-Barreled Monkey Bar Backflip of Fretting."

"That's because it doesn't exist."

Devin snapped his fingers and pointed at me. "Exactly!"

"And what if I just grab you and hold you down until the bell rings?"

"Then I punch you in the face."

I wished I could say that was the end of the story—that I grabbed him, he walloped me good, and it was over with. That would have been so much easier than what actually happened. But how was I to know?

No, I took the phone again, like a good friend . . . like a moron . . . and hit record.

"You're gonna tell me why we're doing this afterward, right?" I asked as I focused in on the monkey bars.

"Totally, bro."

"Probably from your hospital bed."

Devin shivered once, kissed the cross around his neck for good luck, and started the climb.

CHAPTER THREE

GOOD SAMARITAN HOSPITAL, LOS ANGELES

It wasn't just that Devin was my best friend; our families were close, too. My dad had worked for Devin's dad before joining the taxi company, and our moms had met when Devin and I were in kindergarten, since my mom worked at the elementary school. We even had Saturday dinners together at Devin's house. So it was no surprise that everyone rushed to the hospital that afternoon. My parents had picked me up right from school, and we drove over together. Of course Devin's mom was there, but so were his grandma, great-grandma, and great-great-grandma. His sister had been there earlier, even though she was busy with college classes and practices. She had to leave before we got there, which was good for me—Sofia made me freeze something fierce—but that still left a lot of people, and all of us were crammed into the waiting room, eager for news.

Well, almost all of us.

"Addison, where is Devin?" Mrs. Velma asked. "The doctors should be out to update us on his father's condition any second!"

"I dunno," I replied. Almost as soon as we had arrived, he had glared at me, brushed his grandma's hand off his shoulder, and stalked toward the vending machines. That was twenty minutes ago. "Should I go find him, Mrs. Velma?"

"Yes, thank you. And when you do, give him a good, swift kick in the pants for me. Tell him it's from his mother."

"Yes, ma'am," I said softly, and I set out to find Devin.

CHAPTER FOUR

FREEZE UP, LET DOWN

Wandering the hospital halls looking for Devin gave me an opportunity to think about how badly I had let him down at recess.

My first failure had been almost immediate. It was just as Devin lifted his hands into the sky, a silent prayer for safety, that I felt the grip on my wrist. I turned to see Ms. Bazemore's teeth, tongue, and tonsils—that's how close she had come, and how wide open her mouth was as she screamed at Devin. The sound must have shocked him into action, because those upturned hands started flailing around wildly. He fell backward. At that point, completing the DBMBBD was his only option. It was over in a blink, Devin landing on two feet, patting himself and shaking all over. Sure, it was no Maddie Prufrock, but he had survived.

His look of total elation disappeared when he saw me in Ms. Bazemore's clutches. Not only had I been so nervous that I had failed to see her coming, but I had dropped his phone when she grabbed me.

Devin had risked his life.

There was no proof.

And we were caught.

I felt the freeze start immediately, just like it always did. My chest seemed to squeeze inward, ribs and lungs and guts all crowding around my heart, which tried to fight back by pumping as hard and as fast as it could. My hands and feet got cold, my tongue got heavy, and nausea settled over me like the ocean—a big old wave hitting me upside the head while the undertow tried to drag my legs the other way.

Check to see if Devin is okay!

NOPE.

Get Devin's phone before she sees it!

NOPE.

Think of an excuse!

NOPE.

While I stood there, Ms. Bazemore scooped up Devin's phone and pushed him forward. I couldn't move until she turned around, grabbed my wrist, and barked, "You too, Addison!" She dragged us all the way inside, down the hall, and up to the front office.

The *principal's* office . . .

At Ms. Carrillo's door, Ms. Bazemore tried to yell at us, but she was so upset that she never actually completed a sentence. "No phones . . . So dangerous . . . If you had . . . What were you . . . Of all the . . ."

Ms. Carrillo came out to see what the commotion was. Ms. Bazemore could only point—first at Devin, then at me. Flustered, she slapped the phone down into Ms. Carrillo's palm, growled again, and stomped off.

Ms. Carrillo had been the principal at Bennet C. Riley for as long as anyone could remember. She was ageless, it seemed. She kept her hair trimmed so close to her head that she was almost bald; if there was any gray in there, no one could see it. Her voice was never raised, she never smiled with teeth, and her glasses were perched at the end of her nose so that she could always, always look over her rims at you. In the quieter corners of the playground, kids called her "The Immortal."

"What brings you two boys to my neck of the woods?" she asked calmly, like we had just happened by.

I watched her eyes. They roved slowly over Devin, who was scuffing the floor with his shoes. Logically, I knew she didn't have magical powers, but it sure did feel like it. A heaviness crept over the room until her attention settled squarely on me, making my tall self feel about as puny as I ever had. My throat closed.

Good thing, or I might have been sick right there, right then. Devin must have sensed my distress, because he spoke up, and that heavy gaze swept mercifully away, if only for a moment.

"Hi, Ms. Carrillo. I think there's been a misunderstanding. Addi and I were just playing, and Ms. Bazemore came and grabbed us. Brought us straight here. As you saw, she wasn't really in a condition to tell us what we had done wrong."

Ms. Carrillo nodded. "Mm-hmm," she said. "What about this phone in my hand?"

She started to look at me, but Devin jumped in again. "Mine, Ms. Carrillo. I asked Addi to hold it while I played on the monkey bars. I know I shouldn't have it at school, but with my dad being in the hospital, my mom—"

"Child," Ms. Carrillo interrupted, smiling that closed-lipped smile. "How many lies do you think I've heard in my time here?"

Devin shrugged. "Enough?"

She chuckled. "Good answer, and better than the nonsense you were about to feed me. Come inside, boys. Got a few things I want to show you."

She led the way, the slatted blinds over her door clattering as she closed it behind us. Her office was crawling with turtles—stuffed, plastic, hand-carved from wood, and curly-cornered watercolor ones that kids had painted for her. She even had a real turtle in a tank just beneath her window. His name was Fanny, which was short for Ceiling Fan, which was what happened when you let your grandkid name your turtle. She brought him to all our assemblies. Ms. Carrillo beckoned us over to the tank, and at first I thought she was going to show us something in there. Or maybe feed us to Fanny. Instead, she pointed out the window.

"What do you see, Addison?" she asked.

Answer her!

NOPE.

Devin stood on his tiptoes.

"It's the playground, Ms. Carrillo."

"Good, Devin. That was a bit of strategy on my part. When the school was built in '72, I told the architect to put my office in this very spot, told him to put the window exactly where you see it now. And I told him to build the playground right out there. Know why?"

Devin nodded.

"And know what I saw, just now?"

He nodded again. "The truth."

"Just so, boys. That was the first thing I wanted to show you. Second thing'll take me a minute to find. You sit down over there. I'll be with you directly."

As she turned to rummage through a filing cabinet, Devin snapped his fingers to get my attention. I was so nervous that I almost ran—anything to get me out of there, to let me breathe a little. But again, my legs wouldn't do much, only letting me shuffle over to the chairs, clear away a turtle pillow, and sit. He kept pointing and bobbing his head toward his phone. Then he mouthed, "Did you get it?"

A fresh wave of sweaty shame rolled up my neck and across my cheeks. I shook my head. His eyebrows lifted, then knotted in anger. I looked at the floor. The rug was turtle shaped.

"Ahh. Here we are," Ms. Carrillo said, holding a stack of file folders in one hand and keeping her glasses steady with the other as she read. "Yes. The . . . oh, what do you all call it? The Double-Barreled Monkey Bar Backflip?"

"Of Doom," Devin added.

"Yes," Ms. Carrillo agreed. "That's the one."

She sat down at her desk, clearing a few other papers away. Then she tossed one of the folders down emphatically in the empty space.

"Jenny Tapale, 1988. Three broken fingers."

She slapped the second one on top.

"Xavier Rodriguez, 1994. Dislocated left shoulder."

Three more followed, one after the other.

"Mark Newendeis, 2003. Fractured fibula. LaToya Norris, same year. Seven stitches in her lower lip. Erin Marks, 2008. Broken jaw, four lost teeth."

Ms. Carrillo stood up, pressing her hands to the stack of files. She leaned toward us, leveling that laser-beam gaze. "See where I'm going with this, boys?"

Devin nodded quickly, like most kids would. She was expecting the quick nod.

My teeth just chattered.

"Devin, you got lucky. Absurdly, ridiculously, inconceivably lucky. Don't get me wrong—I'm glad you didn't get hurt. But in some ways, you pulling this stunt off is worse than if you'd been the newest addition to that stack. It's important to me, boys, that you understand why. That's the goal here; I'm not going to punish you. Heck, I'm even going to give you your phone back, Devin . . ."

He scooted forward in his chair.

"At the end of the day."

He slumped back down.

"But first I want to hear it from both of you. Can you think of a reason why old Ms. Carrillo might be concerned about what you've done? You tell me that, and I'll let you go with a warning. A stern one, no doubt, but a warning."

I glanced desperately at Devin, hoping he'd answer for us. Before he could, though, she said, "Addison, you first. You were the one trying to film the thing."

I had failed as a watchman. I had failed as a cameraman. This was my third failure. It wasn't even like I didn't know the answer. I did. It was right there, all big in my brain. I squirmed in my seat. I felt the sweat in my socks.

Say it!

NOPE.

"Hmm. I see," Ms. Carrillo said. "Perhaps you two *do* need a bit more of a consequence, so that—"

"It's a bad example!" Devin blurted. "I get it, Ms. Carrillo, and Addi . . ." He scowled at me but continued. "He gets it, too. Because I pulled it off, other kids might try it. Then they'll get hurt, and you don't want to see more kids added to that pile."

Ms. Carrillo sat down at her desk again. "That's right, Devin. Lord, if this school didn't always have two dozen other things to pay for, I'd have had those monkey bars ripped out a decade ago. As it stands, I'd like your help making sure nobody else tries what you did. That means not talking about your success. That means warning other kids to put the idea out of their minds. And that means never, ever doing it again."

Devin agreed, and he tugged me out of there by the arm. I slumped down against a couple of lockers, not even caring that the handles scraped my back. Then I pulled up into as tight a ball as I could, and I tried to calm down.

A while back, Mom and Dad took me to a doctor. She was the one who told us about exposures, and she recommended some ways to help when I froze. Most of them didn't work, but there was one that kind of did. She called it "countdown to countdown," or something. I just called it "thawing." With eyes closed and teeth grinding, I took myself through the tiny steps.

Count to five!

NOPE!

Count to four.

NOPE.

Count to three?

Okay.

One, two, three . . . Breathe.

When I could open my eyes, I searched for Devin, but he had already marched off. That was all right; I wasn't in any condition to talk to him, even though I owed him an apology.

A big one.

CHAPTER FIVE

DEBTS AND TRESPASSES

I spotted Devin's sneakers sticking out from between the hospital's soda machine and the one that sold prewrapped sandwiches. There couldn't have been more than a foot and a half of space in there, but he had wedged in good. He had always liked tucking himself into tiny little places.

"Devin?"

"Go . . ."

"Do you want to talk about it?"

". . . away."

I peeked into the crack. He was staring down at his phone, his face as scrunched as he was. I gave his sneaker a little nudge with mine.

"Hey, look. I'm sorry. I know I let you down. But it was a dangerous thing to do anyway, and I figure we got lucky—"

"It was my only plan, Addi! I'm back to square one! And I've lost all this time, thanks to you. I should have, like, a thousand followers and ten thousand views by now. Would, too, if I had that video. But I'm stuck on zero!"

"Followers? Views?"

The screen of his phone illuminated his face as he looked up. "Yes. Followers. Views. You know, Twitter? YouTube?"

I wasn't sure if the anger I saw in his eyes was better than not seeing his eyes at all. Still, he was talking to me. That was progress, right?

"You have a Twitter account? Don't you need to be, like, sixteen or something for that?"

"Thirteen, and I'm almost there, so I figured I could create one. By the time anyone does anything about it, I'd be the right age anyway."

"Why do you need a Twitter account?"

"Helps you advertise," he mumbled.

I waited for more of an explanation, but he just stared at his phone. I sighed. "Look, I'm sorry. I owe you big-time. . . ."

"Damn right you do."

"But your mom told me to kick your butt if you didn't get back to the waiting room. We're about to find out how your dad is doing."

Devin scrunched farther in, until his back pressed up against the wall. "You'll tell me how it goes? I've got more work to do here."

I shook my head. "I'm not joking, and neither was your mom. She actually told me to give you a kick in the pants if you didn't come."

"Good luck getting that big old foot back here, then. I ain't coming. 'Specially not with you."

He was right. I couldn't fit back there. But I had long arms, so . . .

"Hey! Leggo my foot, Addi!"

I tugged until he started sliding out of his little nook. He dropped the phone in his lap and reached back to grab the corners of the vending machines. With his other foot, he kicked at my hands. It hurt, but I didn't let go. At least, not until a nurse came out to see what the commotion was.

"What in God's name are you two doing?" the woman demanded. She was tapping her foot impatiently, and her huge pouf of black hair bounced in time. I let go; the lady might have been smaller than me, but her arms were crossed, and they were thick. Devin's great-grandma had arms like that. They were the arms of a woman you don't mess with.

"Um, I . . ."

I froze, is what. Bunch of NOPES battling in my brain. Devin used the opportunity to wriggle around in his hidey-hole. His head popped out like a gopher with glasses.

"I dropped my phone, miss!" he declared. "I went in to fish it out from under the Coke machine, and my buddy was reeling me back. See? Got it!"

He held up his phone as he slipped free and stood. The nurse muttered for a second, but Devin gave her that crooked, killer smile of his, and she started laughing.

"Well, now that you've got it, stay out of there. There's wires and plugs, and I'm not so sure the janitors clean back there."

"Yes, miss," Devin said. As she walked away, Devin elbowed me. "And you owe me *again.*"

Once I had thawed, I kicked him in the butt.

"Hey!"

"Your mom's orders," I said, holding my hands up and stepping back.

"Funny. I'm still not coming."

I grumbled, "You have to. It's your dad, Devin! Not to mention the rest of your family, and mine. We've got to be there."

I grabbed at the phone, but he jerked it away too quickly. I said, "Seriously, dude."

He said, "Yeah, seriously," and looked up at me. He was teary-eyed.

"Whoa," I murmured.

"Addi, you're telling me that you'd want to be there if you were me? If your family was cursed like mine was? I can't go in there. Not with him hooked up to all those machines, all that expensive equipment."

"I thought you said you didn't believe in the Curse."

Devin waved his hand around, indicating the wings of the hospital.

"Yeah, well, maybe now I'm not so sure."

CHAPTER SIX

THE VELMA
FAMILY CURSE

It did make sense, I suppose—not that his family was actually cursed, but why Devin might talk about it that way. His family history was a little strange. Even my mom and dad spoke about it sometimes; Mom called it *uncanny*. Dad used the word *creepy*.

I thought they were both right.

For the past five generations, the men in the Velma family had passed away young. Like, really young. Devin's grandpa died when he was thirty-one years old. His great-grandpa made it to thirty-three, but his great-great-grandpa only lasted to twenty-eight. Apparently, there were even more early deaths going further back, and all for different reasons. That's why Devin wasn't surprised when he found out his dad had had a heart attack at age thirty-nine. He was upset, sure, but not surprised.

It was his great-great-grandmother's idea to call it a curse, and once she started, the rest of the grandmas did, too. They were maybe the wildest part of all this: while the Velma men died young, their wives lived on. I didn't know any other kids at school who even had great-grandmas, let alone great-great ones. And for all of them to live in the same house? Let's just say Devin was lucky not to show up for homeroom every day with his cheeks pinched Santa Claus red. And he never, ever came to school with his shirt untucked. It's probably why he got so good at talking his way out of stuff—lots of people to practice on.

First there was Devin's mom. She was thirty-eight, supersmart, and worked for Devin's dad's company as their accountant. Anything on your math homework you needed help with, she was your go-to. Devin's grandma was fifty-seven. She was the cook of the family, and boy, could she *cook*. Owned a restaurant for a while. Devin called her G. That was helpful, since there was also Double-G and Triple-G in the house, too. Double-G was seventy-nine, and Triple-G was ninety-six. Of all of them, I liked Triple-G the best, because she told the funniest stories, cared the least when we snuck candy before dinner, and could do all kinds of amazing tricks and practical jokes with her dentures. She also cussed the loudest at the TV when the Rams stank up the joint.

It was Triple-G who came to find us, the rubber tip of her cane squeaking as she twisted it on the tiled hospital floor.

"There y'are!" she huffed. "Your daddy's been out of surgery for ten minutes and hasn't seen his little man. Go on. Get back there and hold his hand or something."

"He's . . . he's okay?" Devin asked. His words nearly got lost in his smile, it was so big.

"Yep. Curse doesn't have him yet."

Devin shoved his phone into his pocket and rushed down the hall. As I watched him go, I held my hand back to see if Triple-G wanted help to the recovery wing. Quick as ever, she whipped out her false teeth and put them on my palm. When I screamed and dropped them, she laughed so loud the nurse came out again.

"Got you, boy!" Triple-G said, her words surprisingly clear for a ninety-six-year-old with her teeth on the floor.

I picked up her dentures, ran them under the nearby drinking fountain for a second, and watched as she popped them back in. I couldn't help but smile. Triple-G was awe-some like that.

And, along with my parents, she was one of the few grown-ups who didn't make me freeze.

"So Mr. Velma didn't have another heart attack?" I asked when she took my hand for real.

"Nah. There's *something* wrong with his ticker, though. You should've seen him, Addison. He was pastier than a vampire, and his feet swelled up like cantaloupes. I thought the darn things were gonna pop, maybe spray us all with pus 'n' toe jam."

"That's really, really gross, Triple-G."

She cackled in reply and poked my foot with her cane. "Yep! Try getting that one out of your head anytime soon, boy!"

Normally, she'd have had me; it'd take me days to get the image of a vampire melon with toes out of my head. But as I led Triple-G down the hallway, all my other worries crowded in. I had witnessed my best friend do the Backflip of Doom. We'd been taken to the principal's office. I had frozen. Twice.

It had been an exhausting day, and it wasn't even dinner-time yet.

CHAPTER SEVEN

MR. VELMA

It turned out that we were each only allowed a few minutes in Mr. Velma's room—doctor's orders. Devin, my dad, and my mom had already been in and returned to the waiting room, as had G and Double-G. Triple-G and I were the last ones to visit. Still, Mr. Velma smiled broadly when he saw me, and he held up a little plastic controller in his hand.

"See me squeezing this, Addison?" he said. "That's me hugging you. Thank you for coming, and for chasing down my son. I hear it took some effort to get him in here."

Mr. Velma was a hugger; I think that's part of the reason his furniture company did so well. If you bought a couch or a bed frame or a TV stand from Mr. Velma, it came with a hug, free of charge. Not being able to wrap his arms around everyone was probably harder for him than the actual surgery.

"No worries," I managed. Unable to help myself, I stole a quick glance at his feet. Fortunately, they were under a blanket.

"Well, it means a lot. And you've already been in here longer than that son of mine. What's gotten into him?"

I wish I knew, I thought. Instead, I muttered, "The Curse?"

"Curse nothing!" Mr. Velma laughed. "Bad genetics, maybe. But I ask you, Addison: Am I dead?"

I smiled. "No, sir."

"Precisely. If anything, this proves there is no Curse!"

"Oh, there's a Curse, all right," Triple-G said. "But it isn't on you lot. More like it's on the Velma women, cursed to eternal widowhood! I can still remember the day my husband died, all wheezy and hacking with the flu."

I lowered my eyes and took Triple-G's hand again. "I'm sorry."

She shrugged, her dark, wrinkled neck pulling in like a startled earthworm. "Don't be. Wasn't the flu that killed him; it was trying to paint the house while he was sick. Coughed so hard he fell right off the roof. Dummy."

Mr. Velma laughed again, even though it clearly hurt.

"Oh, Great-Great-Grandmother . . . it might be a curse to you, but it is more like our blessing! We Velma men are everlasting, because we marry strong women with minds like steel traps. We shall never be forgotten—you lot won't let us!"

"You bet your one good ventricle we won't," Triple-G stated.

"Addison," Mr. Velma said more softly. "Have they told you what's happening with me yet?"

I shook my head.

"Two weeks ago, right after my heart attack, the doctors said there was a chance I might have more complications. Congestive heart failure, it's called."

When he saw my eyes widen, Mr. Velma held up a hand.

"That look—it's the same one my son gave me. It's not as bad as it sounds. My heart hasn't failed."

Triple-G's knuckles cracked as she squeezed her hands tight on the knob of her cane. "It's bad, though. Don't sugarcoat it."

Mr. Velma sighed. "She's right. It means that my heart is having trouble beating on its own. I started feeling the symptoms yesterday, and today's procedure confirmed it."

"Can they fix it?" I asked.

"They can, but it's another major surgery, and they'll have to put a defibrillator and a pacemaker in. Life isn't going to be the same as it was."

"That's assuming you can even afford it," Triple-G grumbled.

Mr. Velma ignored her.

"I talked to Devin. He didn't say much, but I can tell he's worried. Addison, you'll keep an eye on him? Find him, make sure he's okay?"

"Yes, sir," I promised. Mr. Velma's news explained a lot, but I had more questions for Devin anyway—about his plan, and about how I could make today up to him. It was time for some answers.

CHAPTER EIGHT

DEVIN'S PLAN

Devin was slouched in the corner of the waiting room, his feet propped on the back of one chair, his head and shoulders on the seat of another. He was frowning at his phone, grumbling, "C'mon . . . c'mon!"

I swatted his feet, and he nearly fell down. As I twisted the chair to sit next to him, he shoved my shoulder.

"Addi! Can't you see I'm concentrating?"

"Don't care. Twitter isn't as important as your dad. He wants me to make sure you're okay. You get how ridiculous that is? Guy is in the hospital for the second time in two weeks, and he has to ask if *you're* okay?"

"Yeah, well, this isn't working like I thought it would."

He sat up and looked around like a seagull getting ready

to swipe something. His mom and mine were across the room, hunched over some insurance paperwork, and my dad was keeping Double-G company by playing cribbage with her. If Devin whispered, there was no way they'd be able to hear him.

"Look."

He showed me the screen of his phone. His Twitter page was open. Devin pointed to the upper left-hand corner, where it said, "Following: 357." Next to that, it said, "Followers: 0."

"Nobody knows you, I guess," I said.

"That's the problem!" Devin shouted. That got his mom's attention. She shot him her best "Don't make me come over there" face. He grinned nervously and gave her a thumbs-up to calm her down.

"That's the problem," he repeated in a whisper. "I'm following all the famous people I can think of, but nobody's following back. If I could just get, like, one celebrity to follow me, then other people might, and I might get famous."

I snorted.

"No, man. For real! That's how I'm going to save my dad. That's how we break the Curse, if there is one."

"I don't get it."

Devin scooted in closer. I could smell the orange soda he had been drinking.

"See our moms over there? Know why they're tearing their hair out?"

I glanced. "Uh, forms?"

"Money, dude. The doctors said my dad needs a procedure."

"A pacemaker and defibrillator, whatever those are."

"Yeah. To help his heart pump. Without them, the doctors think he has, like, six months to live. Max. And our crappy insurance won't pay for them."

I winced. "Whoa. I'm sorry, Devin."

He sniffled, but then sat up straight, punching the arm of the chair as he growled. "But I'm going to save him."

I thought about reaching out to put a hand on his shoulder, but he seemed so tense I thought he'd scream if I touched him. Instead, I just asked, "How?"

"My dad can't work anymore. He can't even lift ten pounds. Mom has to take care of him, and my sister doesn't make enough money to help. So I'm gonna earn the money."

I instantly thought of my older brother, Marcus. When he was our age, he mowed lawns and weeded gardens. The money he earned was enough to save up for a computer before he went away to college.

"How much do you need?"

"Eighty-five thousand dollars, at least."

I nearly fell out of my chair. There wasn't a lawn big enough in all of L.A. for that.

"Do you know what the real Velma Curse is, Addi?" Devin asked.

I shook my head.

"You should come to the graveyard with us one Sunday. Try walking through all these huge monuments, with flowers and carvings and stones bigger than you. Some of the people in there even have mausoleums. Know what those are?"

I shrugged. "A dead-guy thing?"

"They're entire *buildings* dedicated to dead guys. Think about it—a whole building, just for you."

"I bet the dead guy doesn't care much."

Devin growled. "That's not the point, man. The point is walking through all that, only to get to the row of lonely little stones with the name *Velma* on them. Every Sunday afternoon, Addi. It's church and lunch and the graveyard with the Gs. My family has been doing that for years. My dad.

My grandpa. My great-grandpa. All of them my age, walking through the monuments of people who lived for sixty years, for eighty years, for one hundred years, just so they can stare down at their dads' graves. Well, that's not gonna be me. I'm not losing my dad for a long, long time."

I nodded, then sighed. "But that much money? It's impossible."

"No, it's not!" Devin insisted. "We can do it!"

I shook my head and tried to reply, but he cut me off.

"Remember the Gold Rush?"

I was a kid in California. We all remembered our lessons about the Gold Rush.

"Yeah, but unless you've found an old mine in your backyard, we're not—"

"Pssh, no. It's this, Addi." Devin held up his phone. "The internet. This is the new Gold Rush. Look. Tell me how many followers I've got now."

"Still zero."

"Damn it!"

From across the room, Devin's mom cleared her throat loudly. Devin rushed to make the sign of the cross, then kissed his necklace.

"Devin," I said, "you're not going to get rich that

way. You've got to, like, be a singer or an actor or a basket-ball player or president. Something like that. That takes tons of hard work and practice. Steph Curry shoots five hundred shots a day, and he does the same dribbling exercises—"

"I don't want to hear about your dumb Warriors right now, Addi. Besides, it's totally possible. I'll show you!"

Devin furiously typed something on his phone, and in a couple of seconds he was showing me somebody else's Twitter profile.

"See the number next to followers?"

I did. It was almost eight million.

"This guy got that many followers just by playing video games and posting the videos online. That's eight million people who know him, who listen to what he has to say, and who will buy anything he sells. Endorsement deals for days!"

"How many followers does Klay Thompson have?"

"Will you stop with the Warriors already? You're in L.A. Be a Lakers fan like everyone else."

I backed away and glared at him. "Says the Clippers fan."

"Hey, my sister works for them. I've got family alle-giances. That's why I'm doing this, remember? And besides,

I'm not a bajillion feet tall like you are. I'm not going to get rich by being in the NBA."

"Or the NFL, or the NHL, or Major League Baseball, or—"

"Yeah, yeah. I know. And I don't have time to learn a musical instrument."

I snickered. "Well, we all know you can't sing. Remember the fifth-grade talent show?"

It had been the highlight of the whole year. Devin had gone onstage to perform a rap that he had written—or, as he had announced it, a "debut of golden lyrics and diamond vocals." He had on sunglasses, a hat turned backward, and just about every necklace he could steal out of his mom's jewelry drawer. The best part was that he made Mr. Turnbow, the music teacher, introduce him as "Lil' Swaggy D." When the curtains opened, he basically started spitting on the microphone and jumping up and down, screaming a poem he had written for a sixth-grade girl he had a crush on. She got so embarrassed that she ran out of the auditorium. When Devin saw that, he stopped his routine, dropped his sunglasses an inch down his nose, and said into the mic, "She's just stunned by the swag." We all busted out laughing. Anyone else would have crawled off the stage. Devin made it seem like a triumph. The judges gave him the award for best solo act. Of course, it helped that I had agreed to be one of the judges; he had bugged me for weeks to join him onstage, but there was no chance.

"Bro, I owned that," Devin said, crossing his arms.

"That's true, that's true," I conceded. "But it's not exactly top-of-the-charts stuff."

"So you see why I had to come up with another way. And I've found it. That video game guy? He posts clips of himself playing games on YouTube, and he tells people about them on Twitter. Then a bunch of people watch his videos, and he rakes in the cash. I did the math. A thousand views means seven or eight bucks. Ten thousand views? Eighty dollars. A million? Eight *thousand* dollars. And ten million? Ten million views, Addi, can get us there. It can end the Curse."

"Ten million views? That's . . ."

"Not as many as you'd think. This guy posts a video a week, and he gets five million views for each of them. Some guy from Korea makes dance videos and gets *billions* of views. And it can happen like that," Devin said, snapping his fingers. "The new Gold Rush."

"But you're not famous. How are you going to pull this off?"

Devin shrugged. "My plan was supposed to have three phases. First, get an amazing video. The right one will hook people—you know, someone will watch it, then tell their friends about it, and it'll spread."

"A viral video," I whispered, thinking of the time Devin and I had sat around all afternoon, watching clips on YouTube of a kid shoving his finger into his brother Charlie's mouth, and more of a poorly drawn duck bugging a guy for grapes.

"Exactly. Get the right video, and you can get millions of people watching within weeks. Second, get Twitter followers so I can advertise my videos and rack up more views. Third, profit. But phase one didn't go so well," he muttered, scowling at me.

"I said I was sorry. Like, a hundred times."

"Then prove it. Help me."

My first instinct was to say no; that afternoon had gone badly enough. But Devin was on the edge of his seat, hands wringing around his phone as he stared at me. His thick glasses made his eyes seem much bigger, and there was no missing the tears that welled there.

"Fine." I sighed. "What do you need from me?"

"Yes!" Devin hissed. "First, I need you to promise not to tell our parents what we're doing."

I crossed my arms. In all the books, movies, and TV shows I'd ever seen, "Don't tell our parents" ranked right up there with "What could go wrong?" and "Well, it can't get any worse" as the biggest jinxes.

"C'mon, Addi. You remember what happened when I tried to make a lemonade stand in third grade."

"You wanted to put it on the side of the freeway in the middle of a traffic jam!"

"It was ninety-seven degrees out! We would've made bank, Addi, if my mom hadn't stopped us. But she put her foot down, so there's no way she'll let us try this. That's why you have to swear you won't tell."

I shook my head, but I swore.

"Great! Next, sign up for Twitter and follow me. You can be, like, my first fan, and the first step in phase two!"

"Um, what? No. Dude—I can barely take people following me in person."

"You don't even have to look at it after you sign up. Think of it like writing your name on a wall, then walking away. You'll never know how many people have seen it, or written their names below it, or anything. It's just there, even though you don't have to be."

"I know how Twitter works. I just don't want to be on there."

"Please?"

My shoulders slumped, and I twisted the blue-and-gold nylon of my jersey around in my hands. I knew that having an account on something like Twitter wasn't like standing in front of the entire world, but something about it didn't feel right. It was kind of like the lake at summer camp. I could watch fifty kids swimming in the muddy brown water, but that still didn't mean I had made peace with the sharp sticks, snakes, and snapping turtles that could be in there. I guessed I had to decide which was worse: the burn in my belly at the thought of trying Twitter, or the ache in my heart at the thought of disappointing Devin.

"I'll . . . I'll ask my mom and dad tonight," I said.

"But you won't tell them why, right?"

I nodded, and he smiled.

"Thanks, Addi. I knew you'd come through for me. Now hush so I can get to thinking about a new phase one."

He patted my shoe and went back to peering at his

phone. I squirmed silently in my seat. He thought he was getting his first follower, courtesy his best friend.

If he had been thinking straight, he would've known exactly what a cop-out "I'll ask my mom and dad" really was.

CHAPTER NINE

THAT STUPID
DISHWASHER

"**M**om," I asked as we drove away from the hospital that night, "can I use the computer when we get home?"

She held up a finger, the nail still painted green from last week. That was one of the things she did for kids in her class. When it was someone's birthday, she'd paint her nails the kid's favorite color the night before.

"Dad?"

"Shhh. Your mother's on the phone," he whispered. I sat back and watched the meter run. Normally we would've taken the bus, but Dad had said it was worth taking his taxi to make sure we got to the hospital in time for Mr. Velma to wake up. I wasn't so sure. I thought it was a rip-off that we couldn't use it for free, but that was the new company policy, apparently. They'd made a lot of new company policies recently.

"That's right, Ms. Rhodes. He can't come back until he's nit-free and the school nurse checks him. I'll make a homework folder for him tomorrow; you can pick it up at the front desk. Yes. Mmm-hmm. You have a good night, too, and sorry about Eric. Don't forget to wash those pillowcases."

My mom set the phone down on the dashboard and shuddered.

"Lice again, Mom?"

"Fifth case this year. Fifth!" she mumbled, and she started scratching at her scalp. I kept my hair buzzed close, but I started itching, too. Couldn't help it.

"Mom, I was gonna ask—"

"I heard you, yes. What do you need the computer for?"

I paused. It's not like I could lie; the computer was right there in the kitchen, big old clunky monitor out where everyone could see. They didn't let me on unless they were in the room, either. "Too many creeps out there," my dad said.

I didn't like my chances, but I had promised Devin to at least try.

"I need to sign up for Twitter. Devin's on there, and he needs me to follow him."

Dad reached up to grab the rearview mirror, angling it so that he could see me. Or, more likely, so that I could see his eyes. He glared at me, then took a deep breath like he was going to give a big speech.

Mom beat him to it.

"Are you serious, Addison? You're twelve. You don't need a Twitter account, and quite frankly, neither does Devin. There's a reason you don't even have a phone. I see my students with them, and they cause nothing but headaches. And don't get me started on that whole 'What if my baby needs to reach me because of an emergency?!' nonsense. Trust your teacher, that's what. We've been keeping kids safe without cell phones for hundreds of years. Why does little Johnny or Susie suddenly need to call every time they scrape a knee? Ridiculous!"

"Yeah, but, Mom, I'm not asking for a phone. I just need to help Devin out. I'll sign up, follow him, and then never check it again."

"Addison, sweetheart. You're his friend in real life. You were there for him today when his father got out of surgery. You're always there for him. That's enough."

"K, Mom," I said.

"Good boy," she replied, and she kissed her fingers and pressed them to the wire screen between the front seat and the back. Sheepishly, I kissed my hand and held it up to hers, just like we always did. I wondered if she'd be so quick to call me "good" if she knew I was using her to weasel my way out of helping Devin. At least this way, I had an excuse about why I hadn't signed up.

We dropped the taxi off at the company garage, then caught our usual bus home. By the time we got in the elevator to head up to our apartment, it was eight o'clock already. My stomach was rumbling so loud my parents could hear it.

"You ate a snack at the hospital, right?" my dad asked.

"Two," my mom responded. "I gave him money, and he came back for more."

"What? I'm always hungry. I'm a growing boy!"

"Don't remind us. You're on your third pair of shoes since the start of the school year!"

And I needed another, I thought as I looked down at my sneakers. I had already had to replace the laces twice, and the heel of the left shoe was coming unglued. That was the price I paid for playing basketball every day on the blacktop. Well, that and all those scrapes on my elbows and knees.

My shoes thumped on the carpet as we headed toward our apartment, and I tried to keep the heel from flapping too much. If the third pair had irritated my dad, the fourth would drive him ballistic.

Kind of like the big brown envelope leaning up against our door.

Before he even touched it, my mom clicked her tongue. "Just let it go until tomorrow morning, Matthew."

My dad had never been particularly good at letting things go. He snatched the envelope up and swiped his finger underneath the seal. As soon as he pulled the first sheet of paper out, he was cursing under his breath.

"Maybe wait until we're inside to blow a gasket?" my mom said, unlocking the door and pushing my fuming father in.

I followed him into the kitchen, trying to get a sense of what was in the envelope. I had only seen the top of the crisp white paper. It was stamped with the symbol of Los Angeles County, and it said: "From the Los Angeles County Department of Public Works." The whole way, my father was grumbling. He didn't even stop to put his bag down.

He just tromped over to the phone, snatched it up, and started dialing.

I paused at the huge hole in the floor, the one between the sink and the stove, and looked down. Ms. Culverson was in her kitchen making a pot of tea. She glanced up and saw me, and I blushed. I felt safe talking to our downstairs neighbor, but still got the prickles at the back of my neck, even so.

"Sorry about the noise, Ms. Culverson," I said. "My dad got some kind of note from the government."

"Hopefully a response to his letters about the landlord?"

I shrugged. "I don't think so. He's madder than that."

Ms. Culverson smiled. "Well, I'm sure it'll all get worked out. In the meantime, I can't say I mind the company, even if it is staring down at me from a messy hole in my ceiling. Here, Addi. Lemon cookie?"

I looked up at my mom, who rolled her eyes but nodded. It's not that she didn't approve of Ms. Culverson and me talking through the hole, or even passing cookies. It was the hole itself that was the issue. I grabbed the cookie and shoved it in my mouth. I really was starving.

"Thanks, Ms. Culverson," I said, covering my mouth to make sure I didn't spit crumbs. "And thanks, stupid dishwasher."

The stupid dishwasher—that's where the hole came from. When we had first started renting the apartment, my mom had been thrilled that it had a working dishwasher. "Nothing worse than wiping the noses of twenty-six eight-year-olds, only to come home and have to wipe grease off dishes for an hour," she had said. It didn't matter to her that it was old, or that it made a ton of noise. It got the dishes clean.

Of course, it should've mattered. We knew that now. The noise, it turned out, was the high-pitched whine of air and water being forced through a crack in an old bit of rubber hosing beneath the dishwasher. That water and air gradually ate away at the wood and plaster beneath the dishwasher until finally that poor floor just gave up, dumping a big mound of damp drywall and piping onto Ms. Culverson's kitchen table. It was a Friday evening, so I was home, and when I heard the crash I rushed to the kitchen. The bright light of Ms. Culverson's apartment beamed through the dust and darkness, as if an old '49er had gone digging in our kitchen and struck gold. I scrambled over to the hole and looked down. Our grubby dishwasher was hanging by pipes and hoses right over the middle of Ms. Culverson's Friday-night poker game, kind of like the world's worst chandelier. Nobody got hurt, but once the dust settled and the shock wore off, Mrs. Hanamura from apartment 7B threw her cards up at the ceiling and declared, "I fold." The next day, we had to get a crew in to remove the dishwasher before it did any more damage.

So now we had no dishwasher, a hole in our kitchen floor, and a heaping helping of trouble. It turned out the landlord wouldn't accept responsibility—we hadn't reported any problems with the dishwasher before then. My dad had argued that we hadn't known about them, since all the damage was hidden beneath the dishwasher, but the landlord got our neighbors to testify about the noise, and he said that was grounds to force us to pay for the repairs. The insurance company wouldn't cover the damage either; they required a note from the landlord to even get in and assess the damage, and he wasn't about to write one. Of course, Ms. Culverson was nice enough to offer to pay for the repairs, "On account of that I should've said something about the water stains on my ceiling a long time ago," but my parents wouldn't hear of it. That left us stuck in a great big hole, so to speak.

And now it seemed like that hole was about to get deeper.

"They're closed!" my dad moaned.

"Well, of course they are, Matthew. Nobody's open at eight o'clock at night!"

"What's wrong, Dad?" I dared to ask.

My father threw the envelope onto the ground in reply. It skidded toward the hole, and I stomped on it. Picking it up, I was able to read quickly before my mother grabbed it from me.

"No way," I said. "They think we violated the drought restrictions?"

My mom scowled as she read on. "Apparently, the leakage from the stupid dishwasher caused us to go over our water limit four times in the last six months."

"Wouldn't that show up on our water bill?"

"We don't pay it, Addison. The landlord does, for the whole building. He just adds a bit to the rent to cover it. L.A. County was probably sending him letters, and he ignored them until now, when it's convenient for him to report us. According to the government, we're on the hook for the fine, which is ridiculous. Do you know how much water we'd have to use to warrant a fine this high? We'd have to be filling bathtubs. The landlord is just using this as leverage."

"That's gotta be . . . ," I began.

". . . Illegal!" shouted Ms. Culverson from below. "Sorry. Couldn't help but eavesdrop! Anyone else want lemon cookies?"

I bent down to get another one, but my father shook his head.

"Sorry, Ms. Culverson. We'll keep it down. Have a nice night," Mom said in her "This concludes our parent-teacher conference" voice.

"You too, ceiling-neighbors!"

I spent the next five minutes scrounging together some dinner while my parents whispered to each other. It kept Ms. Culverson from catching anything, but I picked up every word. Not that I needed to hear. I knew they were talking about money. My parents only ever whispered about two topics: finances and love, and this didn't seem like a particularly romantic moment. Either way, it wasn't something I wanted to stick around for, so I grabbed my sub sandwich and hightailed it to my room.

I shared my bedroom with my brother before he went away to college. Now I used his bed to eat on and mine to sleep—fewer crumbs on my comforter that way. In a weird sense, he was mixed up in all this, too. He was the first Gerhardt man to go to college, and his tuition was on my parents' "nonnegotiable" list. A fourth pair of shoes for Addison's huge feet? Negotiable. Our own car? Negotiable. Marcus's college money? Nothing doing.

That's why I felt fine eating on his bed. After all, what with the stupid dishwasher and these new fines, it might not be too long before sandwiches were negotiable, too.

CHAPTER TEN

DEVIN'S FIRST FOLLOWER

Bennet C. Riley was in a decent neighborhood. It took up a whole block if you included the teachers' parking lot, the playground, and the fields, and it had nice-looking palm trees on each corner. Across the street was a public park, and if we were lucky, a few food trucks would set up over there around three o'clock so we could get a snack while we waited for the bus.

Before school started, a bunch of us camped out on the stone wall in front. There were maybe three dozen kids in all—so many that the school started sending Ms. Rosa to keep an eye on us. It used to be that when I perched on the wall, I could get a good, rhythmic kick going with the heels of my shoes. Now my feet scraped the ground.

That morning, I sat with Benji Wilson. He was a fourth grader with redder hair and more freckles than anyone else I knew. He claimed he could see the freckles on his nose if he crossed his eyes just so. He told us he counted them every day, and every day there was at least one more.

"Hey, Addi! What's your guess today?"

I shrugged. "Seventy-one?"

"Ninety-two! That's up one from yesterday. Mom says it's 'cause I'm growing. Watch out. Gonna block your shot soon!"

I looked down at him. He was beaming. I didn't have the heart to tell him I was still growing, too.

"Maybe so, Benji."

I scanned the street for Devin. His grandma usually dropped him off out front before she went into the market, but I figured they might be late, what with his dad and all.

"Hey, Addi! Did you hear that Devin did the Backflip of Doom yesterday?"

My feet stopped kicking.

"So cool! I'm gonna try—"

"No, you're not," I said gravely. I turned to face him,

putting my nose so close I thought a freckle might hop on over, just to spite me. "It was dumb of him, and it would be dumb of you, too."

"Awww, but, Addi . . ."

I imagined Ms. Carrillo standing over my shoulder. "No, Benji. And you're going to do me a favor. Anyone else says they're going to try, you tell them Addison said it was off-limits. You got it?"

Benji swallowed, but he agreed.

"I guess it's pretty dangerous, huh."

"Very."

We sat there for a few moments more. Another bus full of kids pulled up, and Ms. Rosa directed them to open spots on the wall, away from the street.

"Hey, Addi!" Benji exclaimed suddenly.

I sighed.

"Yeah, Benji?"

"So you're in a hole, right?"

My mind immediately conjured Ms. Culverson's face, smiling up at me from the floor. I arched an eyebrow. "Huh?"

"Yeah, Addi. You're in this hole, right? And there's two ways out. Way A and way B. Which way do you take?"

"Is this a joke?"

"It's a riddle! My teacher told it to me yesterday."

I shrugged, but it was better than Benji talking about the Backflip of Doom again.

"Are the two ways different?"

"No, you don't get to ask questions about it. You just pick!"

"If they're both ways out, does it matter?"

Benji scrunched up his nose.

"I dunno. My teacher didn't say that part. Have you picked one yet?"

"I pick A."

"Wrong! It's B!"

"Okay," I said, and I reached down to mess with some of the concrete along the top of the wall. If you got your fingers under there just right, you could pry up a nice, flat piece of it.

"Don'tcha wanna know why?"

I looked at him again. He was twitching, and his eyes were wide, like he was going to explode in freckly fireworks if I didn't humor him.

"Why?" I asked.

"Because when you're trying to get out of a hole, you

always take the latter! Get it? *Latter*? Like *ladder*? You climb out with the latter. Or ladder. Because it's like the second choice, you know?"

At just that moment, Devin snuck around from behind us. He must have been dropped off while I was contemplating Benji's facial constellation.

"Devin!" Benji exclaimed. "You did the Backflip! Was it hard? Were you scared? How did you pull it off? You're, like, a superhero!"

Devin glanced around, then grinned. "You heard? Man, it was awesome. I pretty much—"

I coughed loudly and shook my head.

"I mean, um, we're not talking about that, Benji."

Benji pouted, his eyes lowering as he kicked at the wall with his sneaker and shoved his hands into his pockets. Suddenly, though, his head popped up.

"Hey, Devin, so you're in this hole . . ."

"Wha?" Devin asked, adjusting his glasses.

"Benji will tell you later," I said quickly, hopping down and dragging Devin through the gate toward the school.

"What's up, Addi?"

"We need to talk."

"Totally. I've got news!"

When we snuck behind the bushes under Mr. Ruffalo's classroom windows, Devin pulled out his phone.

"Check it out, Addi!" he said proudly, and he held up the screen. Between last night and this morning, he had picked up his first follower.

"That's great," I said, "but you need to—"

"You're gonna love this. See who my follower is?"

Devin tapped his screen a few times, and another account came up. In big letters, it said @ADDIGERHARDT17.

"It's you, dude!" Devin proclaimed proudly.

"What? I didn't . . . My mom told me not to . . . I . . . huh?"

"I looked this morning and saw that I still didn't have any followers, and I figured your parents told you that you couldn't make an account. So I made one for you. You're welcome!"

"Delete it, man."

Devin pulled his phone back and cradled it to his chest.

"Heck no!"

"I'll tell your parents, then, and they'll make you delete it."

He started to whimper. "But, Addi, you know how much I need this! How am I supposed to break the Curse if I don't get famous?"

"You mean post a YouTube video."

Devin rolled his eyes. "They're the same thing. Fame gets you followers, which gets you views, which makes you more famous!"

Gritting my teeth, I pressed my fingers to my forehead to think.

"All right. We'll make a deal," I said. "You can keep me as a follower. But we have to leave school out of this. You heard Benji talking about the Backflip."

Devin's shoulders slumped. "So Ms. Carrillo was right."

"Yeah."

"Guess this means you're not going to help me hijack the PA system so I can broadcast my new rap to the whole school?"

I shook my head. "You're kidding, right?"

"Or record me as I try to get from one end of the teachers' parking lot to the other only on the roofs of their cars?"

"Now I know you're messing with me."

Devin pushed a strand of hair away from his glasses and smiled. "Yeah, maybe. But you're coming over tonight to help me think of a new phase one. A real spectacle."

"It's Friday night. The Warriors-Clippers game is on."

"Watch it at my place. Or are you afraid we're going to beat you?"

I laughed. The Warriors beating the Clippers was about the only thing I was sure of these days.

"Then it's a deal," Devin said, and he held out his hand.

I wished I had a pair of false teeth to put in there, just to teach him a lesson.

CHAPTER ELEVEN

A DRAMATIC TURN

My mom talked to Devin's mom after school, and they worked it out so that I could spend the night at his place. To earn the privilege, I had to clean my room until it was spotless . . . or, should I say, crumbless, since Mom had found out I'd been eating on Marcus's bed again. I tried to tell her it was because it made me feel closer to him while he was away, but she saw right through that. I was a terrible liar.

So, after ten minutes of vacuuming and five minutes of trying to pull Marcus's bedspread out of the vacuum hose, I got to call Devin for the pickup. His grandma drove him to get me, and she was standing by the curb when I went outside, an umbrella over her head for shade. I smiled and kissed her cheek, and she stretched up to kiss me back. She was just about Devin's size.

"Good afternoon, Addison," she said warmly. I peered into the car, where Devin was doing . . . well, something. It looked like he was yelling at the back of the driver's seat. Every so often, he'd point at it, open his mouth really wide, and shout stuff. I could hear him even though the car door was closed.

"What's Devin doing?" I asked.

"Same thing he's been doing for the whole drive. He's rehearsing."

"For what, G?"

"Your guess is as good as mine. Let's both hope he stops once you're in the car."

He did, for a few seconds at least. I slung my overnight bag at him, and he caught it and tossed it down by his feet.

"Hey, Devin. Ready to cry tonight when the Warriors stomp your team?"

"None of that from you, young man," G said sternly as she closed the umbrella and slipped into the driver's seat. "It's bad enough having to play chauffeur for the one lonely Warriors fan in all of Los Angeles, but I'll suffer no ill talk about my Clippers. Keep that up, and you're walking."

I reminded myself that I was in enemy territory. The entire Velma family were rabid Clippers fans. Devin's sister was even a member of the Clippers Spirit dance team. I loved G like my own grandma, but I was fairly sure she wasn't bluffing about kicking me out of the car. Depending on what I said, I'd be lucky if she bothered to pull over first.

"Yes, ma'am," I replied. "I meant, 'Devin, are you looking forward to tonight's game? It should be a lively and amusing matchup.'"

"Out!" Devin screamed, pointing at the door behind me. I jumped, banging my head against the ceiling.

"Devin!" G gasped.

"Dude, we trash-talk, like, all the time! What's got you so—"

"Out, out, brief candle! Life's but a walking shadow, a poor player that struts and frets his hour upon the stage and then is heard no more: it is a tale told by an idiot, full of sound and fury, signifying nothing!"

When he was done, Devin was panting. He had been gesturing so wildly that he had accidentally slapped himself in the face, and his glasses were crooked, one lens right above his nose. I could actually see his neck veins pulsing.

"Devin, sweetie, are you not well?" G asked softly. "Because we have some VapoRub at home we could—"

"*Macbeth*!" Devin exclaimed between breaths. "Shakespeare. How was it?"

I blinked. "Um, scary?"

"You were terrifying, dear," G added.

Devin fixed his glasses and slumped into his seat. "I was going for impassioned ennui."

"Impassia-what?"

"Never mind."

We spent the rest of the car ride in silence. I pressed myself as tight as I could against my door, just in case Devin decided to go all Shakespeare on us again.

When we got to Devin's house, he ran upstairs to his bedroom. I stayed to get my cheek kisses from Mrs. Velma, Double-G, and Triple-G; Devin's dad was in bed resting, and his sister was at the arena for the game already. After our hellos, I scrambled up to find Devin.

His door was open, though the light wasn't on. The glow of his computer screen illuminated the back wall, and I could see him furiously flying through websites in the reflection of his window.

"*What* is going on?" I asked as I flung my bag onto his bed.

"Dang . . . ," he mumbled.

I scooted around his desk to look, accidentally knocking over a pile of books on acting. Each one had the familiar public library barcode taped to the spine. At the top of the pile was a copy of the CliffsNotes to *Macbeth*.

On Devin's screen I saw a picture of Disneyland. Above it, a headline glimmered and blinked—it was made entirely of animated stars. Once my eyes adjusted, I could read what it said: "So You Want to Be a Star?" Below that, in regular letters, it continued: "Top ten tips for becoming a Disney child actor!"

I put a hand on Devin's shoulder. "You thought you could get famous as an actor?"

"Look at this!" Devin moaned. "Even this seven-year-old has been working at it since he was two! His parents home-schooled him so that he could focus on acting. How do I compare with Travis Everyoung? That's probably not even the dude's real name."

A fresh-faced blond kid with a gleaming smile stared at Devin from the screen.

"And those definitely aren't real. You ever met a seven-year-old with all his teeth?" I pointed out.

"They might not be, but the twenty-two million subscribers to his YouTube channel are," Devin whimpered as he slid farther and farther down into his seat. "But it's a dead end, too, Addi. Apparently, there aren't actually talent agents just roaming the streets, looking for the next superstar."

"Let me guess . . . You were going to get your mom to take you to Hollywood, then stand in front of the Dolby Theatre and spout lines until someone recognized your genius?"

"Well, yeah, kind of . . . ," he said. "I was going to get you to dress as Lady Macbeth, and then we'd record ourselves. It'd be hilarious and artsy. People love that!"

I stared him down so hard he slithered all the way under his desk. When I grabbed him by the collar of his shirt and hauled him out, he looked up at me with saucer eyes. "Was it really that bad?"

"Worse," I assured him. "Sports, singing, acting—it doesn't matter, Devin. All of it takes work. Lots of work. So you've either got to put in the hours . . ."

"Which I don't have, because of my dad's heart."

"Or know a guy who's famous already who can hook you up. And trust me, I'm not that guy."

Devin kicked at the corner of his desk. "Why didn't my parents make me start acting when I was two?"

"Have you seen your baby pictures? You're lucky they let you out in public with that big old head of yours."

"I grew into it!" Devin pouted. "And besides, why do you have to keep shutting me down? You said you'd help!"

"I am helping, man," I countered. "By telling you this isn't the way."

"Then what is?"

I flopped down on his bed and looked up at the ceiling. There was a picture taped there of a massive galactic battle. Devin and I had drawn it in third grade—*Star Wars* versus *Star Trek* versus the *Power Rangers*. In the center of all these laser beams was Yoda, chopping off Klingon heads and flinging the Red Ranger around with the power of the Force. Usually I felt like Chewbacca, but today I was feeling way more Red Ranger.

"I don't know, but it sure as heck isn't dragging me out to do Shakespeare in the streets. I'm fine right where I am."

"Well, yeah." Devin smirked as he sat down next to me. "As soon as a spotlight hit you, you'd pee your pants."

"You mean like I'm doing right now? On your bed?" I joked, and I smiled wide.

"Ew! Gross, Addi!"

I laughed as Devin chased me downstairs with his pillow.

CHAPTER TWELVE

THE GAME PLAN

Clippers games in the Velma household were a big deal. There was popcorn and ice pops, fruit and chips, and a very specific seating arrangement. The couch that directly faced the TV was occupied from left to right by Mrs. Velma, G, Double-G, and Triple-G. Arranged in front of them were TV trays. Each tray had a plate of food and a drink—a glass of wine, a cup of tea, a bottle of lime soda, and something called a whiskey sour, in that order. Devin, who usually sat on the carpet right in front of the TV, was curled in his dad's recliner. And me? I was on a plastic folding chair next to Devin. "Warriors fans don't get cushions," Triple-G had said.

"That's okay," I replied. "Gonna be standing up cheering so much I won't need one."

"They might have to sleep in the backyard after the game, too," she warned, and I shut up.

The game was awesome—at least, for me. I had plenty of moments where I could have popped my Klay jersey and gloated, but I knew better. Instead I quietly crunched on chips and ate a banana, passing the brown parts to Devin like I always did. The Gs all yelled at the TV and the referees. Double-G even took her sandal off and threw it at the screen at one point. I started to go get it for her, but she barked, "Leave it, Addison. If the refs keep this up, the other one will join it soon enough, and I'll know where to find the pair later!"

It was during a time-out midway through the second quarter that Devin started acting strangely. Well, okay, for him it was acting the same way he had all week, but I knew his brain was chewing on something other than bananas and bad foul calls.

"Wait a sec," Devin said. "Rewind that, Mom."

"Rewind what, baby? It's a time-out."

"Rewinding TV is unnatural!" Triple-G declared.

"It isn't, Mama. All just bits in the stream. Doesn't matter if they're going backward or forward. Why shouldn't you be able to rewind it?" Double-G murmured.

"'Cause it's unnatural!"

I sat back and smiled. Listening to the grandmas argue was maybe one of my favorite things ever.

"Just do it, please, Mom!" Devin begged. He perched on the edge of the recliner, not even looking back. Mrs. Velma rolled her eyes, but she rewound the game a bit, until Devin shouted, "Stop! There! Right there!"

It was still the middle of the time-out, and the camera was panning through the crowd. It had settled on the front row, where a famous comedian was sitting. He eventually noticed the camera, smiled, and tipped his cap.

"Look!" Devin exclaimed. "Did you see that!?"

"What?" I asked. "Billy Crystal? Yeah? So? He's at, like, every single Clippers game."

"No, behind him. And listen to what the announcers are saying!"

Mrs. Velma rewound again, and this time she turned the volume up, too. Behind Billy Crystal were two guys, college kids maybe, and they were going nuts. One of them had an inflatable Clippers hammer and was pounding on the other's head. The second guy seemed not to notice; he was too busy ripping his shirt off to show that he had painted the Clippers logo on his chest.

The announcers seemed unamused.

"And there's the Clippers' number one fan, Billy Crystal, star of *When Harry Met Sally*; *Monsters, Inc.*; and, as far as I'm concerned, *The Princess Bride*."

"Oh, he stole that movie."

"Absolutely did, Chuck, you're right. Hilarious."

"And look at those two buffoons behind him."

"Boy, that really gets my goat—people looking for five seconds in the spotlight by being close to a celebrity."

"I feel bad for Billy, having to deal with those two camera hogs."

"Something tells me, Chuck, that Billy's perfectly content to allow them to have the attention so he can enjoy the game in peace."

"He's probably not enjoying the score right now, with the Warriors up seventeen. . . ."

Devin was watching with his mouth wide open, and he was rocking back and forth a bit.

"There you go, Devin. You saw Billy Crystal. Happy now?"

"Phase one . . . ," he mumbled.

"What, dear?"

"Oh, I mean, yeah, Mom, thanks. Big fan . . . ," Devin said softly. "I'll . . . I'll be right back."

We watched as he slipped out of the chair and skittered upstairs. All four Velma women looked at me. I nodded.

"I'll go check on him."

"Devin's lucky to have a friend like you, Addison," Mrs. Velma said, and she rubbed my back as I walked past.

Upstairs, I found Devin on his computer again. His face was almost touching the screen, and he was reading something fiercely.

"Billy Crystal fan, my butt. I know what you were thinking."

Devin replied without peeling his eyes from the computer.

"Did you see them? How they were on camera and everything?"

"Yeah. But you're not backflipping behind Billy Crystal."

Now he did look at me.

"Pssh. No."

I leaned against the wall behind him. "Good, because that'd be—"

"He doesn't have nearly enough followers. Not even a million!"

I covered my face with my hand.

"So you're thinking . . . what, exactly?"

"Promise to help."

"No."

"You owe me?"

"I already followed you on Twitter."

"No, I used you to follow myself on Twitter. You haven't done squat," Devin said, crossing his arms. Then he started bouncing in his seat like a little kid. He knew I hated it when he did that.

"What are you getting me into? Are you going to streak the court? Please tell me you're not thinking of streaking, because that's a completely different kind of exposure, and there's no way I'm—"

"I don't know what I'm thinking yet, but I know I'll need your help. And this is the way, man. It's free publicity! You saw those two guys! The spotlight! Five whole seconds!"

"I don't think the announcers meant that as a good thing."

"Any press is good press, Addi."

"Not if you get it by doing something stupid, or illegal, or dangerous," I said. After thinking for a couple of seconds, I added, "Or all three."

"What if I swear it won't be?"

I sighed. "I'm your friend. I promised before, and I'm not going to back out now . . . as long as it's not totally messed up."

Devin nodded. "Thank you, Addi. You won't regret this."

I left Devin up in his room, furiously scribbling on a notepad and clicking his mouse. By the time I got downstairs, I already regretted it a little.

At least the Warriors won, 123–111. And I kept my mouth shut so I didn't have to sleep in the backyard.

CHAPTER THIRTEEN

A SIGN FROM HEAVEN

In the morning, I popped my head out of my sleeping bag and looked around. It took me a few seconds to remember that I was on the floor of Devin's room. Part of my confusion came from the fact that I couldn't hear him; he always slept longer than I did, and he snored like an elephant seal with a sinus infection. When I sat up, I saw him. He was at his computer already . . . or maybe, still.

"Tell me you weren't up all night."

"I wasn't up all night." He yawned.

The way he slumped and the red spiderwebs in his eyes said otherwise.

"Wanna go downstairs and get breakfast?" I asked. That banana last night was already a distant memory, and my stomach had more of a "What have you done for me in the last three minutes?" kind of attitude.

"Look, Addi. I've got it," he said, pushing his scribbly notebook at me. I saw a massive cloud of red circles surrounded by more circles. Occasional lines zigzagged through the mess. It looked like a very woolly sheep had exploded onto a herd of even woollier sheep.

"That's . . . nice, Devin. Really pretty drawing! You can tell me all about it after you eat. And sleep. For, like, twelve hours straight."

"Shut up, Addi. It's my plan. The real one this time. Look."

He shoved his rolling chair back from the computer. There on the screen was a picture of a dark-haired woman. I recognized her instantly. Who wouldn't?

"Jeska Monroe?"

"Her most recent music video has almost a billion YouTube views! And it's Jeska Monroe-Stone," Devin corrected. "She's married to Bradford Stone, remember?"

I nodded. It was hard to go anywhere in L.A. without hearing about Jeska Monroe. She had her own TV shows—as in more than one. She was on the cover of every magazine. She sold, like, every product you could think of. At one point last year, she had the highest-rated reality show, the top-selling memoir, and the number one country album in the nation, all at the same time.

Oh, and her husband was one of the most famous actors alive.

I smirked. "Tell me you're not going to hit her over the head with an inflatable hammer," I said, thinking of how ridiculous that would be.

"No. That would interrupt their kiss."

I stopped smirking.

"What?"

"Look."

Devin showed me a series of webpages. The first was Jeska's Twitter page. I saw that she had eighty-eight million followers.

"Whoa . . . ," I whispered.

Then I saw the message Devin had at the center of the screen. It read, "*Got Clips Tix 4 VDAY! SO Xcited 2 B @ game w/ My Man! #Clippers #Valentines #loveislove.*"

"She's going to be at the Valentine's Day game," Devin said, and he pointed to his scribbles. Peering closely, I thought I could make out a letter *V* in there. "Now check this out."

Another Twitter page—Bradford's this time. He had sixty-one million followers.

Devin tapped the screen. "Add that to Jeska's, and you have a hundred and forty-nine million followers. A hundred and forty-nine million, man. That's more than ESPN, LeBron James, and YouTube *combined*. And yes, YouTube has a Twitter account. It's weird."

He didn't look like he was in the mood to have me point out that a lot of Jeska's and Bradford's followers were probably the same people. Still, it was *millions*.

"Now this," Devin continued. The next website was the Clippers homepage. The first article said, "Bring Your B-Ball Baby! Special Prizes Awarded on Valentine's Day for the Kiss Cam Lucky Winners!"

Devin slipped off his glasses, rubbed his blurry eyes, and slapped the notebook. "See? It's all coming together. The Valentine's Day game is nationally televised, Addi. Nationally. And Jeska and Bradford are going to be there. All I've got to do is get to the game, sneak down during the Kiss Cam time, and reveal my message behind them when they kiss. Then we run."

"Your message?" I dared to ask.

Devin leapt up onto his chair, scaring me so bad I stumbled

back onto the bed. He lifted his shirt up just like the guy on TV last night. On his chest and stomach, he had written something . . . a poem, maybe? At least, the kind a twelve-year-old operating on zero sleep might write at three in the morning. It said:

THINK THEY'RE IN HEAVEN?
THEN YOU SHOULD SEE DEVIN!
HIT ME UP ON TWITTER:
@LILSWAGGYD47

"That's . . . that's . . . ," I sputtered.

"Brilliant?"

"Absurd!"

"But not illegal or dangerous!" he countered, jumping off the chair and smoothing his shirt down.

"It might be! It kind of is, to sneak down into the rich people's section! And it's definitely stupid!"

"No, it's not, Addi. At the very least, I get to post a picture of me on Twitter. If you're quick with my phone, we can get a recording to post on YouTube. Sure, I could get into a little trouble, but I'm twelve. And who knows . . . if Jeska and Bradford think it's cute, they might even post links to my videos!"

"I can't tell if this is you trying to break the Curse, or the Curse going into overdrive to get you early. You're gonna be, like, naked in front of the world!"

"Don't be such a grandpa, Addi. Guys do this at games all the time. Remember last night? And it's even less than someone would see at the swimming pool, anyway. Only my belly."

He patted it confidently, like he'd just conquered the Big Fat Fatty sandwich challenge at Fat Sal's Deli.

I trembled just thinking about it. "I'd die before I even got halfway down there," I murmured. "Please don't say you need me to be, like, an exclamation point next to you or something."

"No! You couldn't handle Ms. Carrillo, let alone an arena full of people. Leave the face time to a pro. I just need your help to set it up, and to take video of me with my phone while I do it."

I cringed. "What if I drop it again?"

He rolled his eyes and said, "You won't. Besides, if anything looks like it's gonna go wrong, we call it off. You get to enjoy a game at the Staples Center, and you get to say 'I told you so.'"

"Anything goes wrong at all, and we call it off," I repeated.

He nodded. "Yeah, man. Yeah. We call it off."

I realized I was stuck. What if I shot down this idea, and a worse one took its place? He had already done the Backflip of Doom . . . I figured it was either help him with this, or feel guilty when he tried something even more dangerous.

"If we do this, we're square?" I asked.

He grinned. "Yep."

Wincing, I whispered, "Fine."

"Devin rubbed his hands together slowly, and he pointed down at his hairy wool-pile drawing again. "First, you've got to . . ."

As he told me what I needed to do, I broke out in a cold sweat. I started shaking, and I actually lost my appetite.

Devin wanted me to talk to his sister.

CHAPTER FOURTEEN

DEVIN'S SISTER

This one time, Devin and I snuck into Double-G's bedroom, because he said he had found some books in there we should check out. Double-G was a big fan of romance novels, the kind that had guys with no shirts on the covers. Didn't matter what they were doing or where they were—they had no shirt. Middle of a battlefield? No shirt. Front deck of a pirate ship? No shirt. Standing in front of an entire city while it burned to the ground? Where's your shirt, dude?

In other words, they'd fit right in at a Clippers game.

Devin and I took turns reading out loud all the parts we shouldn't, giggling like fools the entire time. Double-G caught us and scared us away with what I thought was a really, really effective threat: next time, she'd sit us down and force us to listen while *she* read them to us, cover to cover. I don't think I've ever blushed so hard or promised more sincerely never to do something ever again. I even tried to erase from my mind any traces of the stuff we *had* read, just so I wouldn't have to imagine it in Double-G's voice. Still, no matter how hard I tried, a few details stuck. One of them was how every book seemed to talk about the woman in the story. It was weird, if you thought about it: they all called the ladies "indescribably beautiful," and then went on to try to describe them anyway.

Well, Sofia was not that. She went so far beyond that, she circled right back around to *describably* beautiful. Devin liked to tease me about having a crush on her. He couldn't have been more wrong, though. I didn't have a crush on her.

I was terrified of her.

Whenever I saw her, I froze. Of course I did. But it was different, because with her, everything shut down *except* my mouth. It was like the NOPES wanted to make me embarrass myself as much as possible. She'd say, "Good morning, Addison!" and I'd just start describing: "Your hair is dark and shiny and like waterfalls of oil only not the greasy kind I mean the kind that you can see all the colors in on the blacktop after a car pulls away and I think that's really pretty and you're pretty too."

So I avoided her whenever I could.

That morning, though, I couldn't. We needed tickets to that Clippers game, and according to Devin's plan, Sofia was our way in. It made sense—she had been asking us to come see her dance all season, and she had team connections that could get tickets any time we wanted. The trouble was, Devin couldn't ask her. He could smooth-talk just about anyone, but his sister always saw through him. She'd know he was up to something.

Add that to the fact that he had ruined a pair of her yoga pants last month by using them to make a giant slingshot, and he was on the outs. That left me.

When I peeked around the corner into the kitchen, I saw her. She was standing at the counter eating fruit salad. Immediately, my mind broke.

Turn around and walk away!

NOPE.

Hide behind the doorframe!

NOPE.

Say hello as awkwardly as you can!

SURE!

"Hi morning!" I squeaked.

Sofia turned to look at me and smiled.

I almost collapsed.

"Heya, Addison! What did you think of the game last night?"

She reached up to brush a strand of her hair from her eyes. Her fingernails shimmered with purple nail polish.

Run!

NOPE.

"I . . ."

Say you liked the game. Say you liked the game. Say you liked the game.

"I . . . like . . . your nail. Nails. Fingernails. You have nice fingernails, and the Warriors won. The Warriors won, which means the Clippers lost, and you dance for the Clippers. I'm sorry. You shouldn't clip your fingernails, by the way. They're purple like grape juice."

She giggled. I grabbed on to the kitchen counter for dear life.

"It's okay, Addison. Did you want some fruit salad? Something else? Mom's not awake yet, so if you and Devin are hungry, I could whip up something before I head out to my Saturday-morning class."

"No fruit salad," I croaked. "Tickets."

"Tickets?" she asked.

"Not for breakfast. For the game, on the fourteenth. Valentine's Day. To see the Clippers play the Hornets. Three tickets. Please."

I closed my eyes, then opened one just a crack to see if she understood.

"You guys want to come see me dance? Addison, that's great! We get a few blocks of tickets set aside for family and friends each game. I'll claim mine for that night! I was worried nobody'd be able to come this year, what with Dad's heart and everything. You've totally made my day, big guy!"

Then she glided up, kissed me on the cheek, and walked out of the room.

Last year, I passed out once. It was right after basketball practice, and it was incredibly hot—like, wring the sweat out of your jersey and watch it evaporate on the concrete hot. Coach had us doing suicide sprints, and after five sets, I wasn't feeling too well. When I sat down, my vision got blurry, like someone had shaken up a Coke and poured it into my eyes—little black fizzes and pops starting from the outsides and filling up everything I could see. I woke up five minutes later with Coach holding a wet cloth to my head. Heat exhaustion, he said.

This was definitely another Coke-in-the-eyeballs moment.

The next thing I remembered was Devin leading me to a chair, sitting me down, and pouring me a glass of water.

"You're totally pale, bro," he said. "Are you gonna throw up?"

"I did it," I whispered.

"What? You threw up?"

"I did it," I repeated, louder. "I got the tickets."

"I knew you could do it! Did she figure out what we're trying to do?"

"I don't . . . I don't think so."

"What seats did you ask for?"

I blinked.

"Seats?"

"Yeah. Like, what row? What section? We talked about this, remember? It's gotta be someplace where I can get down to the front row before the third-quarter TV time-out. That's when they do the Kiss Cam."

"Row? Section?"

Devin slapped the table. "Addi! Duh! If you didn't tell her what seats to get, you're just going to have to talk to her ag— Addi? Addi?"

Coke.

Eyeballs.

YUP.

CHAPTER FIFTEEN

THE DEVIN IS IN THE DETAILS

"**R**ow fourteen, section three-nineteen! Are you kidding me?!" Devin screamed. He had the tickets in his hands, and he was moving them back and forth in front of his face. I think he expected the numbers to change if he could only make his eyes focus a certain way.

"Yes, Devin. That's the section they reserved for friends and family of the dance team," Sofia said. Her arms were crossed, and she was tapping a foot impatiently. I was squeezed up on the recliner, my knees pressed to my mouth so that I wouldn't give in to the urge to tell her how well she pulled off "effortless irritation," or something equally dumb.

"But it's so far from the court!"

"Yeah, you'd think that in addition to our minimum-wage salaries and our nonexistent benefits, they'd give us courtside tickets with the players' wives. What were they thinking? I'll just call up the owner right now and tell him there's been a mistake."

"Really?" Devin asked, his frown instantly replaced by a sugar-sweet smile.

"No, Devin! Of course not!" Sofia shouted. Then she narrowed her eyes. "You know, little brother, I'm beginning to think something's going on here. I know you don't care about the Hornets, and it has never mattered where you sat before. What are you playing at?"

"Nothing!" Devin said, unblinking. "Addi mentioned during the Warriors game that he wanted to see you perform, and I said he should ask you if we could go! Right, Addi?"

My eyes nearly popped out of my skull, I stared so hard at Devin. I couldn't tell whether to be furious at him for bringing me into it again, or impressed that he was able to lie so smoothly. I think I managed to move my head enough to make it look like a nod, though.

Sofia puffed a curl of hair out of her eyes. "Well, whatever your reason, those are the tickets you've got. You're stuck with them. And I expect you to watch our performances. All of them, Devin."

"Fine, fine," he said, and he turned back to his phone as he waved her away.

When she was gone, I uncurled myself. My knees and ankles cracked, I had been balled up so tightly.

"That was close," I muttered. "She knew something was up."

"Look," Devin said, and he pointed to his phone. I leaned down to squint at the screen. There was a map of the Staples Center arena, and Devin had zoomed in on our row and section. It was up really, really high—what my dad called "the nosebleed seats." The court, and Jeska and Bradford, were going to be tough to get to.

"We'll have to leave our seats . . . ," Devin paused, whipping out a pen and doing some more exploding-sheep calculations. "At the very end of halftime. Probably need to sneak around to the Eleventh Street entrance side, make our way down, shoot between one-thirteen and one-fourteen, then cut across. You'll need to stand on the other side of the court to get the picture, so we'll split up right behind the press section, here." He pointed again to the map. It all looked like colored blocks to me; I hadn't been to the Staples Center since Devin's ninth birthday party, and I wasn't very good at remembering places like that.

"And what about security? Won't they check our tickets when we try to get into the better sections?"

Devin tapped his temple. "Another reason why we're headed down at the end of halftime. Everybody's getting back from the bathroom and concession stands. With that many people moving, we should be able to slip past."

"And if we can't?"

Devin stood up, squinted, and pointed off in the distance.

"There, mister! Down there! I see my parents. They have my ticket. Want me to go get it and come back to show you?" He smiled. "Right? They're not gonna make you bug your parents and bring a ticket back, and they don't want to deal with an angry mom or dad, so bingo."

"Speaking of angry parents, what do we do when . . . Wait, who's bringing us to the game again? I could ask my dad."

"No. It can't be him. Probably my mom, or maybe G."

"Why not my dad? I think he'd like to see the game, and between my mom and him, he's the least likely to strangle me for trying this."

"Because of the BBS."

"The what?"

"Bathroom buddy system. That's how we get away from whoever brings us to the game. I say I have to use the bathroom. My mom would never let me go alone, so she'd demand that I take you with me. Problem solved. If your dad is there, he might come with us, and we'd never get away."

"And when we don't come back until after the TV time-out, and your mom sees you on the Kiss Cam pulling your shirt up?"

Devin shrugged. "I'm not worried about that part. If I get to Jeska and Bradford, I've already won."

"Assuming Bradford doesn't see you behind his wife and chuck you right out of the Staples Center."

"Are you serious? That would be even better! Think of the pictures we'd get!"

I shook my head.

"And there's nothing I can say to get you to drop this whole thing?"

"Not unless you rip that Addi face mask off, reveal that you're actually Jeska Monroe-Stone, and let me take a picture of you with my belly."

So that was a no, then.

Devin socked me in the shoulder playfully. "Don't look so nervous. Maybe you did blow it on the playground, but I've already forgiven you. You got the tickets, right? And sure they're crummy, but we'll manage. I have total confidence that you'll come through for me. That's what we do for each other, remember? Like in kindergarten?"

I nodded. I didn't remember much about Ms. Wentz's kindergarten class, but I did know that even back then, Devin was watching out for me. Maybe he saw some sort of connection—he was the smallest kid in our class, and I was already the tallest; teachers often mistook me for a second grader. One of the librarians even thought I was a third grader once, and she gave me a huge stack of books to take to my mom's classroom. Mom got it sorted out for me, but not before I had missed carpet time and snack. That was a big deal, because if there was one thing I couldn't afford to miss, it was snack.

Part of being so big was that my body was always demanding fuel. It still does, so that it can move these branchy arms and pencily legs around. I probably thought about food as much as the other kids thought about playtime, or about Pokémon. So when my dad forgot to pack my lunch one day in October of '09, it was a disaster waiting to happen.

It didn't have to wait long, though.

Before lunch, we had recess. When I went to my cubby to get my basketball from my backpack, I noticed my brown bag wasn't in there. Right away, I knew how bad that was;

Marielle Brown had forgotten hers three times the week before, and I could remember the pinchy, rhino-faced look Ms. Wentz got when she had to dial up Marielle's parents and have them leave work to bring in food. That had turned into a shouting match, on account of Marielle's mom yelling something through the phone, and Ms. Wentz screaming back about our school's "no-share" policy. By the time the whole thing was done, half the class was crying, and Ms. Wentz stormed out of the classroom for fifteen minutes of "me time," leaving the assistant, Mr. Galbraith, in charge.

It took three Elephant and Piggie books, a puppet show, and two rounds of water in the special butterfly Dixie Cups for him to calm us down.

Desperate to avoid that kind of scene, I scanned the classroom. My eyes settled on the snack closet almost immediately, and my stomach gave me a rumbly thumbs-up. As sneakily as I could, I slipped behind the drying racks and waited for Mr. Galbraith and Ms. Wentz to follow the other kids outside. Then I made my move.

Whoever had built the closet had a pretty good idea—put the handles of the double doors up high where kids couldn't reach them. They just didn't account for me. I strained on my tiptoes, reached up, and snagged a handle, which unlatched and let the blue-and-orange door swing wide.

Before me was a banquet . . . and all of it was colors that I liked to eat. There were the browns, of course, but also beiges, tans, and dull yellows. Not a leaf of green to mar the view. No beet-reds or carrot-oranges or cabbage-purples anywhere in sight. I scanned the shelves, eyes roaming over Cheerios and Life cereal, applesauce cups and pretzel sticks. My plan had been to just grab a few things and take them to my backpack. Yes, it was stealing, but the food was for hungry kids, right?

And man, was I a hungry kid.

Before I could even finger a Frito, though, I heard a commotion at the door. Ms. Wentz was bringing back a group of girls who had forgotten the sidewalk chalk, and I'd only have a few seconds before they'd come in and see me standing there, snack closet open wide. I wasn't even supposed to be inside without a teacher in the first place, so it wasn't like I could just close the closet and back away. No, I only had one place to go.

Inside the closet itself.

There wasn't much room on the bottom shelf, but I crammed in, grabbing the lower lip of the doors and pulling them shut behind me. They locked with a click. I was curled into a tight ball, arms wrapped around my knees and head between my legs like we did for earthquake drills. Even so,

I could see into the classroom through the little crack between the doors. Ms. Wentz hadn't noticed me—if she had, I'd have been yanked out of there faster than I could blink.

So I was safe for now, but I was also stuck.

I'm sure there were dozens, maybe hundreds of times I could have called out, or kicked at the door until someone opened it up and found me. But I was too scared; I didn't want to get into trouble. And being scared? That just made me hungrier.

The bottom shelf, it turned out, was where the Goldfish crackers were kept. They were in these tall cartons, kind of like the ones for milk, only much bigger. I was surrounded by them—my back was even crushing a few behind me. As the other kids came in from recess and started eating their lunches, I realized I couldn't hold out any longer; my stomach was growling so bad that I was worried it'd give me away all on its own. So I started eating Goldfish.

Lots and lots and lots of Goldfish.

It would've been bad enough if I could have just reached into the containers and dug out handfuls of the crackers to shove in my mouth. But no; because of my weird position, I couldn't get at the tops of the containers, and I'd never been good at carton physics anyway. Instead, I had to work my fingernail at the side of one of the boxes until I had poked a hole through. Once I did, I could tear it a bit more until Goldfish started flowing out into my palms.

By the time lunch was over, I had poked holes in every carton that I could reach, eating until too many dumped out onto the floor. Then I'd move on to the next one. My stomach had stopped rumbling, but my mouth was completely dry. I had run out of spit, like, fifty crackers ago, so even if I had wanted to call out for help, I couldn't. I would've just wheezed fish dust all over the place.

It was almost as I had resigned my six-year-old self to living the rest of my life in a snack closet that I heard a little tapping at the door. I moved my eye to the crack and peered out. There was Devin, his huge head and glasses dominating my view. I didn't know him very well at that point, so I started crying, thinking I was doomed.

But I was wrong.

"Hey," he whispered.

"Hey," I managed, crumbs clinging to my lips.

"I could hear the closet munching."

I blushed. "You're not gonna tell, are you?"

"How'd you get in there?"

"Dunno," I lied.

"Are you hiding?"

I nodded.

"Why?"

"I don't have a lunch."

"Ooooh," he cooed sympathetically. I saw him glance back at Ms. Wentz.

"But I wanna get out," I added. My back was hurting where the cracker cartons were poking, and I had to go to the bathroom.

"You're gonna get in trouble."

I sniffled, and new tears came, mixing with the cracker dust on my cheeks to form a sticky paste. My shoes crunched as I shifted in the drifts of Goldfish that had built up around me. "I know," I said after a bit.

"'Cept maybe not."

He smiled, pushing the tip of his index finger in through the little opening. I reached up and touched it with mine. It felt warm.

"I got you, Addison," he said.

"Huh?" I whispered, but he was gone.

I pressed my eyeball right up against the crack, trying to figure out what was going on. I looked over at the sinks, at the cubbies, and at the blocks area, but couldn't see Devin. Then, though, I spotted him . . . he was marching right up to Ms.

Wentz. Terrified, I saw him grab her elbow. She leaned down, her necklaces dangling in front of Devin's face, and followed his finger as he pointed at the closet. Her look of amused concern disappeared instantly, swallowed up by her rhino face.

I tried to shove myself as far back into the corner of the closet as I could, but all I did was manage to crush more cartons of crackers. The doors opened in a rush, and I spilled out . . . along with a tidal wave of Goldfish, like I was the whale caught in the nets that the fishermen were dumping out along the docks. I heard the whole class gasp, two dozen kids all surging forward to crowd around. Mr. Galbraith exclaimed, "Sweet merciful Mary!"

Ms. Wentz was trembling.

"Addison Gerhardt! Explain yourself!" she shouted. I tried to sit up but slipped around in the crumbs and landed back on the seat of my pants, squishing an entire school of Goldfish. I started to respond, but those crackers got their revenge, hiding my voice away in a gooey lump of throat dust.

"Stealing food? You? Shy, quiet Addison? You don't say more than a dozen words in the first month of school, but you'll pull something like this? Wait until your mother hears! I'm going to call her right—"

I wanted to argue. I wanted to tell her I wasn't quiet, or

shy, and that I was only stealing because I didn't have a lunch, but no words came. It might have been the Goldfish. It might have been everyone staring. It might have been my first freeze.

It was definitely Devin's first time bailing me out.

"Um, Ms. Wentz?"

Devin tugged on her sleeve, then did it again, harder.

"Not now, Devin!"

"Ms. Wentz, I think Addison is scared. You shouldn't yell."

All those heads that were staring at me suddenly shifted to Ms. Wentz. Nobody had ever told *her* what to do before. She was so shocked she didn't respond, so he continued.

"Addison forgot his lunch," he said, and four other kids gasped. Marielle started sobbing. "Yeah. He forgot his lunch, and he knew you'd be mad."

"Why would I be mad? Kids forget their lunches, like, daily. Why, just last week Marielle forgot hers so many times that I—"

She stopped, covering her mouth with her hand.

Right there, she had what our sixth-grade vocabulary book would call an *epiphany*.

Because of Devin's heroics, I didn't get into nearly as much trouble as I thought I would. Mostly, Ms. Wentz was sorry. She even baked us cookies to apologize for scaring us. After that, Devin and I were best friends, and he came through for me again and again.

And on Valentine's Day, barring any more surprises, I'd finally have the chance to return the favor.

CHAPTER SIXTEEN

GETTING THERE IS HALF THE FUN

Valentine's Day was full of surprises.

I found out about the first when I got to Devin's house that Saturday afternoon. He pointed at his bed, where there was an outfit spread out on the sheets.

"That's your disguise for tonight," he whispered, and then closed the door behind him, leaving me alone. On his bed were draped a red T-shirt, a Clippers hat, and a Blake Griffin jersey. There were no pants, so I figured I at least got to keep my own. What was there was bad enough, though.

A knock made me jump. "Addi! Are you dressed yet?" Devin asked. It sounded like his voice was bubbling up through the floor—he was crouched and speaking under the door.

"You know I hate Blake Griffin!"

"It's my dad's stuff. I didn't have anything that could fit you. And you're not wearing your Warriors gear."

I frowned, then hunched down to peer at him as he peeked at me.

"Ahh! Scary Addi face!"

"Why can't I just wear my Klay jersey? I wear it everywhere."

"Because you need to blend in to get around security. Wear the stuff on my bed and you'll be camouflaged. Wear the gold and blue and you'll stick out. And probably get beat up. It's pretty much for your own safety."

I pushed myself up and took off my Klay jersey, shoving it beneath the door to block Devin's view. I could hear him giggling down there, so I stomped on my jersey to keep it in place, and I stretched out to grab the hat, shirt, and Blake Griffin top. In a few seconds I had it all on, the totally flat brim of the hat cutting across my forehead uncomfortably.

When I let Devin in, he sized me up.

"Decent. Could you maybe pretend like it wasn't burning your skin to wear it?"

"I'm not that good of an actor," I mumbled as I reached up to crush the brim into a more comfortable curve.

"Hey! You're ruining it! Straight across is the style!"

"It'll look more worn this way, like I've been a Clippers fan all my life," I argued. "And it's easier to hide under here." That was the key. Anything to keep me from freezing in the middle of a basketball arena.

"Fine," Devin grumbled, but he didn't stay mad for long. He bounced down the stairs, skidded on his socks through the kitchen, and was at his mom's side before she could even put out a hand to slow him down. He bumped her into the countertop. Because she was on the phone, she flashed him an angry look and put her hand right on his face to push him away. I listened in to her conversation.

"How much longer, Ma? No. That's no good. We told you we needed the car by five o'clock to get down to the game."

Devin drooped like someone had pulled a cork from his ankle and let the excitement drain out.

"Mom. Mom! Do we not have the car?" he whined. She put her hand over his mouth, but he swatted it away.

"Fine, Ma . . . No, you stay there," Mrs. Velma said into the phone as she held Devin at bay. "We'll . . . I don't know. We'll think of something. No, Sofia already took the other car. No, Ma. You know it's hard to fit in her car anyway, what with all her makeup and gear. Ma, no. Look, I'm going now, Ma. Be safe, Ma. Bye!"

Mrs. Velma hung up and sighed. Devin started whimpering again, but she held up a hand. "Let me think, baby."

After a few moments of pacing, she looked at me.

"Addison, honey, I know you're not going to like this, but maybe Uber . . ."

I shook my head. "No . . . no way. My dad will flip if he finds out. . . ."

"I called the taxi company before this. It'd take them two hours to get a car out here. Apparently, they've cut a bunch of their drivers for the weekend shifts."

She didn't need to tell me. My dad was one of them. He used to be able to get work every single weekend. Now he was lucky to have a shift on most weekdays.

Mrs. Velma put a hand on my shoulder.

"You won't get into trouble. I'll tell him all about it afterward. He'll understand."

I wasn't sure he would. Of all the shouting that had gone on in my apartment over the last year, no word had been spit, cursed, or growled as loudly as *Uber*. Even the stupid dishwasher was a distant second. If he poked at it a bit, I was sure my dad could even find a way to blame the dishwasher *on* Uber.

It was pretty much his version of the devil.

At first, he had said it wasn't going to be anything. "Who

wants to take the chance to ride in some stranger's car when you could call up an experienced taxi driver? You know the rate is going to be fair, you know the driver understands the city. Only a fool would want to take an Uber."

Well, apparently, about three-fourths of Los Angeles were fools, because Uber was raking in the money, and the taxi company was having to hike rates, cut drivers, and change rules. The worst part was that my dad was a loyal, loyal man, but I'd heard him whispering to my mom that if we could ever afford a car of our own, he'd probably have to switch over to driving for Uber, too. That was the devil's temptation, and that's what made him the most angry— where the work was wasn't where his heart was. Still, all he could do was cuss and curse at the new driving service while silently saving up enough money to join it. In the meantime, he had put a strict "No Uber for this family!" rule into place.

Devin tugged at my sleeve. "C'mon, Addi. If there's a taxi outside when the game is over, we'll take that home. Right, Mom?"

Mrs. Velma nodded. I stared knives at Devin.

A Blake Griffin jersey? Taking an Uber to the game?

I had to pull the hat off for a second, just to wipe my

wrist across my forehead. The air-conditioning was on, but I was already sweating, and I could feel my heart thudding against my rib cage. If the sound of my brain ripping joined it, I wouldn't have been surprised. It almost made me *want* to freeze, just so I wouldn't have to get into an Uber.

I consoled myself by thinking of how terrible the driver was going to be. Besides the obvious—horns, red skin, black goatee, little pig hooves for feet—I was sure he was going to get us lost, if he didn't drive us straight off a bridge first. I even decided it would be fun to tell my dad just how horrible it was, and he'd shake my hand for going into enemy territory and bringing back confirmation of Uber's evil. All I had to do was stand on Devin's front porch and watch for a rusted-out black hearse with tinted windows.

When a white minivan pulled up, I snorted. "Gonna need to move that thing so our Uber driver can park," I stated, expecting Mrs. Velma to march down the stairs and tell the cheerful, middle-aged woman getting out of the van to drive on. I crossed my arms smugly as Mrs. Velma did exactly that.

Well, at least the marching part.

My arms dropped when she shook the woman's hand, and my jaw followed when she waved us down.

"Boys, say hello to Mrs. Hutchinson. She's driving us to the game."

"Happy Valentine's Day, boys!" the woman said pleasantly. "There's chocolates and other candy in there. Please, take some. My three kids are all in elementary school. They had their Valentine's parties yesterday, and now it seems like I'm finding Skittles and Smarties in the craziest places. Swear to heaven, my youngest came home trailing Fun Dip powder from her pockets like sand out of an hourglass. She couldn't tell why the dog was chasing her around the kitchen!"

Devin smiled and slid the passenger door open wide. The van was totally clean inside. No wrappers, soda cans, or human skulls anywhere in sight. Even so, I wasn't buying it. As Mrs. Velma and Mrs. Hutchinson continued to make small talk, I tapped Devin on the shoulder.

"Didn't anyone ever warn you about strangers in vans offering you candy?" I asked, pouting.

Devin laughed. "And how many of those strangers hold the door open for your mom while she gets in the front seat?"

I didn't take any candy, on principle. Devin fished around in the bowl until he had snagged all the peanut butter cups. I watched as he methodically bit the bottom halves off each one, then stuck the top halves together to make wheels. These he rolled up and down his tongue until the chocolate melted into a little road. By the time he was done, he was a mess. I glared at him.

"What?" he asked, holding up his chocolaty fingers. "I'm nervous!"

"Worried that the Clippers will lose again, dear?" Mrs. Hutchinson said as we stopped at a light. "I'm sure they'll be fine. Not going to catch my Warriors, though. Is that bad, admitting that I'm a Warriors fan? I just love that Steph Curry. Those three-pointers! Woo!"

Devin slapped a sticky hand over his mouth to keep from saying anything. Mrs. Velma didn't see the problem.

"Oh, Addison back there—the tall one—he's a big Warriors fan."

"Are you really!" Mrs. Hutchinson chirped. "Couldn't tell with all the Clippers gear!"

It was like somebody had suddenly hit me with a huge spotlight. I looked up at the rearview mirror. Mrs. Hutchinson was staring right at my reflection. My throat got tight.

Smile!

NOPE.

Wave!

NOPE.

"He's just wearing that because I made him," Devin said, coming to my rescue. "My sister is a member of the Clippers Spirit, and we're going to see her perform tonight. Family supporting family, and we get to see a game, too!"

"Well, that's lovely!" Mrs. Hutchinson gushed, and the light changed.

The rest of the way to the arena, Mrs. Velma spoke proudly about Sofia: how she was juggling being on the dance team and college; how she had been the salutatorian of her high school class; and about her volunteer work cleaning up the beaches. There were even phone photos shared. The whole time, Mrs. Hutchinson couldn't have been nicer.

And Devin just licked his fingers. Didn't he know I was trying to hate this woman? But she was so *pleasant* . . . and a Warriors fan . . . and not driving us off a bridge.

When we arrived at the Staples Center, I could barely get out of the van. It was bad enough keeping Devin's secret, wearing a Blake Griffin jersey, and having to ride in an Uber. The worst part, though, was that I had nothing I could tell my dad to make this betrayal any easier. Mrs. Hutchinson was just a mom giving rides to help pay the bills, and I wanted to stick a pitchfork in her hands and call her my worst nightmare. An ugly ball of guilt sat in my stomach like the gluey, heavy center of the world's nastiest peanut butter cup. Unfortunately for me, I wasn't going to be able to just quietly melt away on the sizzling sidewalk.

No, there were far too many people for that.

CHAPTER SEVENTEEN

THE STAPLES CENTER

As soon as Mrs. Velma thanked Mrs. Hutchinson, we were swallowed by the crowd pushing toward the Staples Center doors. Devin was wriggling and fussing at his mom, who insisted on holding his hand. I grabbed his shoulder so we'd make a human chain. Eventually, we all squeezed into a line to get into the building.

I kept my head down, shielding my face beneath the hat. I was sure someone was going to point at me and say, "Look! Warriors fan! Warriors fan! Trying to hide in that Blake Griffin jersey!" Then they'd chase me down the street. I tried to get Devin's attention, but he was mumbling to himself. When I leaned in, I could hear him: he was going over the plan again and again. I thought about teasing him like he did to me in the car but remembered that in his mind, this was a life-or-death situation.

I hoped Bradford and Jeska had remembered to come to the game.

"Do you two want anything to eat or drink before we find our seats?" Mrs. Velma asked. "Your mom gave me a twenty, Addison, so don't worry about money."

"I'm good," I replied. Devin was already scoping out the walkways.

"Up there," he said, and he elbowed me. I followed where he was pointing. It was the tunnel leading between sections 113 and 114.

"What are you pointing at, honey?" Mrs. Velma asked. Devin ignored her, his head jerking this way and that as he plotted and planned.

I swallowed. "Um, he . . . he was just saying that right there might be a good place to meet up if, you know, we get separated. Because, um . . . you can see where we came in from there, and there's lots of lights."

Mrs. Velma kissed my cheek, then Devin's. He twitched his nose and wiped the kiss away.

"Good thinking, boys. Way to be safe. Shall we find our seats, then?"

As his mom led the way, Devin continued to bounce around nervously.

"That was a good save, wasn't it?" I asked. He nodded.

"Yeah. Good save. And good plan. After I pull this off, we run. Meet back up where you said. Good spot. Lots of lights. Phase one, right on schedule."

I touched his shoulder, but he shrugged me off.

I'm not going to lie—it would've been nice to have seats down on that lower level. To get to ours, we had to walk around ramp after ramp, then up a dark set of concrete stairs, then up two more ramps, then up two more flights of stairs. When we came out at the bottom of our section, I had to grab the guardrail for a second. No wonder my dad called them nosebleed seats . . . we were up so high I wouldn't be surprised if the air *was* thinner up here.

"Mom, can I have the binoculars?" Devin asked, snatching at her purse.

"Not yet. Save them for when your sister performs. I don't want you dropping them over that edge."

"Please?" he whined, and he started hopping up and down.

"No. And be careful. These steps are slippery."

I knew why Devin wanted the binoculars. It was hard to

see the people sitting in the first row. There were a few couples who seemed like they might be Jeska and Bradford, but it was impossible to tell for sure. I leaned over the guard-rail a little to look and immediately regretted it. Below us were the luxury and press boxes. They formed a sort of wall around the middle of the arena, like they wanted at least forty feet of distance between the people who paid for good seats and, well, us. It was the kind of drop I could imagine Gage and his buddies spitting off of, trying to land one in somebody's drink cup. I backed up, and I pulled Devin away with me. His mom was already halfway up the rows.

"Here we are," she said when we reached her. "Row fourteen. One thing's for sure, we'll definitely be able to see Sofia's performance from here."

"Yeah," I said as I sat down. "We just won't be able to see Sofia."

It was already loud, like the music was being pumped in right above our heads. Across the way, people were stream-ing down the aisles and filling seats. It reminded me of a game of Connect Four, how they trickled in and filled up the plain black seats with red shirts and jerseys. It didn't hurt that they seemed to be about the size of checkers, either.

The huge jumbotron screens hung from the middle of the arena ceiling like the world's biggest bats. They flashed highlights of the 2016–2017 Clippers—DeAndre Jordan dunks, Chris Paul crossovers, and J. J. Redick threes. Some of the plays were from games against the Warriors. I winced whenever they showed Blake Griffin posterizing one of my favorite players.

"Mom. Mom! Can I have the binoculars now? Mom?" Devin begged. He reached over to slip his hand into his mom's purse, but she slapped it away.

"But, Mom, I need to . . ."

I grabbed Devin's arm and shook it.

"Not now, Addi! Mom! Why can't I have the binoc—"

"Devin!" I whispered.

"What?"

I pointed at the jumbotron. They had stopped the highlights and were showing the players stretching and warming up. Just behind where Jamal Crawford was running a cut drill was the first row of seats. Right there, dead center, was Jeska Monroe, and next to her sat Bradford Stone. She was on her phone, and he was turned around shaking a fan's hand, but there was no mistaking. It was them.

Devin pulled his hand from his mom's purse, no slapping necessary.

"Mmm-mhm! I do love watching those players str[…] Maybe I'll use the binoculars first, eh, Devin?" Mrs. V[…] said.

Normally that'd be when Devin would start his [...] puking noises. I had to jump in on his behalf.

"Ew, Mrs. Velma," I muttered.

She laughed mischievously and lifted the binocula[…] nudged Devin.

"Bro, things are *not* good when I have to start cove[…] for you."

"They're actually here. This is really happening, Ad[…]" he whispered.

"It doesn't have to. We could say we tried it and it di[…] work. We'd still have that story to tell, like the Goldfish [...] the Backflip."

Devin shook his head and scratched his belly. This ti[…] the story wasn't going to be enough.

CHAPTER EIGHTEEN

THE PRIDE OF THE VELMA FAMILY

I'd never been less interested in the score of a game in my life. I tried to watch the action, tried to get into the music, tried to do the wave as it came around, but none of it seemed to help. Despite all that color, all that noise, my eyes were glued to the plain little flashing bulbs that counted down the quarter. Devin was just as nervous—he passed me his phone in the first minute and mumbled, "Be ready."

My hands were so shaky I nearly dropped it, just like I had on the climber. It was dumb, but I couldn't help looking around for Ms. Bazemore . . . and we still had more than an hour to go before the third quarter started.

At least there was the end of the first quarter to look forward to. That was when Sofia and the rest of the dance

team performed their big number. Mrs. Velma was so excited she didn't even notice how uncomfortable we looked. In fact, she was closer to the edge of her seat than we were, and she was yelling at the refs about each foul call, no matter who it was on. Fouls stopped the clock, after all. There was one play when DeAndre Jordan left his feet to dunk the ball, and a Hornets player grabbed both his arms and yanked him to the ground. Mrs. Velma was irate.

"C'mon, ref! Let them play!"

The guy in front of us turned around and stood up. He was so big that his head was at Mrs. Velma's level, even though he was a whole row down.

"Hey, lady," he said, his voice booming. "Who're you rooting for here?"

Mrs. Velma didn't even look at him.

"I'm rooting for these sweaty men to get off the court so I can see my baby do her thing!"

He arched his huge, bushy eyebrows and looked at me. I shrugged.

When the final seconds of the first quarter did run down, all three of us counted them out loud. As the players grabbed towels and Gatorade, the dance team ran to center court, leaping and twirling. From what I could see, they just looked like little pieces of red candy—something out of Mrs. Hutchinson's bowl. There was no way I could tell which one was Sofia.

Then they showed up on the jumbotron.

Sofia was slightly to the left and back, a tall blond girl partially obscuring her. Immediately, Mrs. Velma screamed, "Get that supermodel wannabe outta the way!"

The big guy glanced back. I shrugged again.

Their performance involved lots of hips, lots of kicks, and enough hair whipping that I was pretty sure I felt the breeze up in section 319, row 14. The dancers shifted halfway through, so I could actually see Sofia. That meant watching the clock wasn't an issue anymore. My eyes were glued to the jumbotron screen.

It was a good thing, too. If I had been looking at the timer, I might not have paid attention to the end of the routine. . . .

Or heard the terrible, terrible announcement right afterward.

As Sofia and the other dancers clapped and waved at the audience, the announcer said, "Let's hear it for our Clippers Spirit dancers! What a way to ring in Valentine's Day, right? And speaking of Valentine's Day, the Clippers would like to invite you to celebrate this special day in a special way, with a very special edition of our Kiss Cam! That's right, folks: no need to wait until the third quarter. Get ready to pucker up for prizes!"

The jumbotron screen went black. Then a border of pink and red hearts popped up, a wide shot of the crowd at the center. As the camera zoomed in on one couple, a blur passed in front of my eyes.

"Devin!" Mrs. Velma screamed. "Where are you going?"

I shot up, too, only just remembering that Devin's phone was still in my lap. I fumbled with it for a second before catching it.

Not this time, Addison, I thought, and I smiled.

Then I dropped the phone into the big dude's lap anyway.

Devin was tearing down the steps.

The slippery steps.

He was tearing down them way, way too fast.

I bolted after him, my legs eating up the stairs five at a time. I could feel my old, floppy shoes threatening to break apart, they were hitting the concrete so hard.

It didn't matter, though.

Devin stumbled, skidding down the final few steps. He tried to turn but couldn't.

He flipped over the guardrail, just before I slammed into it.

Devin fell.

CHAPTER NINETEEN

THE FALL

I didn't think. I didn't stop. I just lunged.

And I caught Devin by the leg.

It was the worst pain I'd ever felt in my life. My fingernails scraped along his calf as he slipped, and I could feel the nails pulling away from my fingertips even as I dug them in. Devin was screaming. So was I, bent at the waist over the guardrail, and I would have tumbled right after him, but my long legs had wedged underneath the seats of the first row behind us. If I had been any shorter, or Devin any heavier . . .

It seemed like forever that we stayed that way, my hands wrapped around Devin's ankle, him flailing beneath me. It was so loud—the music, the shouting, the gasps from the entire arena. Before I could even think to look for help, I felt it: dozens of hands on me, longer arms reaching next to mine and grabbing my hands, grabbing Devin's shoes, his feet, his legs. As the people behind us came to our rescue, I was pulled back and upward, but I refused to let go of Devin.

No way was I letting go.

Not even when they yanked me back far enough that I could see the jumbotron, my own face broadcast all huge and horrified, Devin still dangling beneath me.

CHAPTER TWENTY

THE FALLOUT

With the help of all those hands, I hauled Devin over the guardrail. I fell backward, and he landed on top of me. I wrapped my arms around him because he was shaking so hard.

We were surrounded immediately. The people who had been helping just a moment ago tried to pull Devin off me. They touched my hair, my shoulders, and my legs. I closed my eyes and tangled up around Devin like an octopus. When I did, that image from the jumbotron flashed in my mind. I had caught him with one hand. One hand, five fingers, and forty feet between him and the concrete below.

"Addison!" I heard, a shrill voice cutting through. "Addison, baby! You can let go now! It's over!"

I peeked, and Mrs. Velma was there. She had pushed the other people back, and she was tugging at my arms so she could get to Devin. I peeled them off, revealing the tight little ball he had curled into.

When he saw his mom, Devin climbed into her embrace. She rocked him, and from the floor I could see the blood on his leg. My fingernails had dug big gouges in his skin before I got a better grip. I looked at my right hand. The nail on my index finger was torn up pretty bad, and the one on my middle finger was just gone. It was bloody and gross, and I had to look away.

It wasn't long before I felt someone hoist me up. My legs were wobbly, but I managed to stand. Four security guards in fancy red jackets pointed toward the tunnel entrance while they talked on walkie-talkies, and they formed a circle around us to lead us out. We were hustled along the hall, past staring people, past clapping people, past people taking pictures. Soon, the guards moved us into an emergency medical room, where they had us sit on exam tables covered in crinkly white paper. A gentle lady with her hair up in a net knelt in front of me, taking my hand and dabbing at my fingertips with a cotton ball covered in orange liquid. It stung badly.

"You!" the biggest of the security guards shouted, pointing at me. "What happened up there?"

Answer him!

NOPE.

Breathe!

NOPE.

Anything?

ABSOLUTELY NOPE.

The man looked angry. His teeth were grinding, and he was very sweaty.

"I slipped," Devin said, his head lifting off his mom's shoulder. "I slipped and Addi saved me."

"That guardrail is tested. Only way someone your size goes over it is if you're running straight at it, or you try to climb over. What were you thinking?"

Mrs. Velma responded before Devin could. "Does it matter? He didn't fall. We're not going to sue, if that's what you're worried about. I just want to get these boys home."

Another guard shook his head.

"I'm afraid that's going to be difficult, ma'am," he said, then held up a finger while he brought his walkie-talkie to his ear. After a moment, he glanced nervously at the other guards. "They know. Gonna be thick around the door."

"Who is?" Mrs. Velma demanded.

"The press. Your boy picked a hell of a time to throw

himself off the edge. National TV game during the audience pan for the Kiss Cam. They got it all on the broadcast. Game is delayed until they find out whether or not the kids are okay. I'm supposed to radio the head of security so he can make an announcement to the crowd. So?"

"So?" Mrs. Velma retorted.

"So are they okay?"

"My leg hurts," Devin said, and Mrs. Velma hugged him close again. The nurse looking after him was slathering his leg with the orange stuff, too. She paused, putting her gloved hands on her knees and looking up. "He'll be fine. His friend's hand got the worst of it."

The gentle lady was wrapping a bandage around my middle finger. "This poor guy is going to be smarting for a while. Nails are slow to grow back, but he'll live. He should be taken to the hospital, though, so that they can get this properly tended to, maybe get X-rays just in case. We don't have the equipment here."

My fingers throbbed in time with her words. Mrs. Velma came over and rubbed my head.

"We'll get you to the hospital, Addison. As soon as we're out of here, I'll call your parents. They can meet us there."

"Quiet, please," the security guard barked, and then he

growled something into the walkie-talkie. A few seconds later there was a rumble through the arena.

"Just made the announcement. That was the crowd reacting to the news that you're okay."

We *were* okay. I took a deep breath. Devin wiped at the corners of his eyes. I didn't remember him crying, but I couldn't blame him.

The security guards asked Mrs. Velma bunches of questions, and they had her sign all these papers, too. A dozen stadium officials poked their heads in, whispered to the guards, and then disappeared. After a while, I caught Devin's eyes, and he hopped off his table to join me.

"Your hand looks like she mummified it."

"I can't move my fingers," I replied through clenched teeth—even talking to Devin, that's still all my brain would allow.

"You saved my life."

"I guess so."

"I'm sorry."

I nodded. "And I'm sorry you didn't get to show your belly. But at least it's over."

He scooted away from me, his eyes wide. "Over? No way! I nearly died out there, Addi. Do you know what that means? Think of the viewers! It's happening!"

I gaped at him.

"Tell me you didn't go over the guardrail on pur—"

"No!" Devin gasped. "Of course not! But you heard the guard. The press is outside, and they caught us on camera. We can use this! Just follow my lead."

When the guards opened the door, it was difficult to follow much of anything. We were stuck; reporters and more security bunched around the door like kids around a playground fight, all of them climbing over one another to catch a glimpse of us. I tried to hide behind Mrs. Velma, but that was no use.

"What happened up there?"

"Can you tell us if you were pushed?"

"Did you jump on purpose?"

"Hey, tall kid! Great catch!"

"Hero! Hero boy! What did it feel like to save your friend's life?"

The questions came so fast I couldn't figure out who was asking them. As we pushed through, the squishy ends of microphones kept bumping against my face. I wanted to swat them away, but I had to keep my hand tucked close to my chest—if my fingers accidentally hit something, I would have screamed. Fortunately, the security guards muscled up, and with Mrs. Velma's stern face leading the way, we managed to make it out of the crowd.

Almost.

Just before the exit, a reporter yelled out that she was from ESPN. Devin stopped, worming his way out of his mom's grasp. He turned around and said, "Hi, ESPN! I'm Devin Velma. D-E-V-I-N V-E-L-M-A. That was the scariest thing that's ever happened to me, but thanks to my buddy, I'm safe! Follow me on Twitter, and check YouTube!"

Then he tugged his shirt up.

I'm not sure anyone saw his message; Mrs. Velma corralled him so quickly that I thought there might be a Devin-shaped hole left in the air, like in cartoons. We basically ran to the parking garage. Sofia was waiting with the car; she had been given permission to leave the game once she had found out it was her brother who nearly fell. She rushed up to us, her heels clicking on the pavement. First, she threw her arms around Devin. I could see she was crying.

"You're okay!" she gasped.

"Yeah," he said. Her eye makeup was getting all over his cheek, and he tried to wipe it away.

"What were you thinking, you stupid, stupid boy?! You could've died!"

"I was trying to come see you after your performance, and—"

"Liar. You're such a liar," she hissed at him. "Stupid!"

Then she hugged him again.

Once he wriggled away from her, she pressed her palms to her eyes. They came away gooey with mascara.

"Ugh, I'm a mess, but I don't care. I'm going to hug you, Addison. Come here," she said, sobbing again. I just stood where I was. She grabbed me anyway. "Thank you, Addi. You saved my baby brother."

Respond like a fool!

OKAY!

"No problem. Anytime."

She laughed and snorted—perfectly—and opened the car door for me. I ducked in and closed my eyes; I felt suddenly very, very tired. I think I would've even fallen asleep if I hadn't been sitting on a tube of lipstick. Mrs. Velma had to reach behind from the front seat to nudge me when my parents called.

"Addison! We saw the footage on the news! How are you feeling?" my dad asked. He sounded very cheerful, like how he talked to his customers in the taxi. That's how I could tell he was worried about me.

"I'm okay, Dad. They're taking me to the hospital for my hand. Will you be there?"

"Yes, Addison. We're already in the car. The Velmas picked us up. We're all on the way to meet you."

"All of the Velmas?" I asked, imagining my dad sandwiched into the backseat of the Velmas' sedan, right between Double-G and Triple-G.

"Yes," he said. "All of them. Including Mr. Velma."

"Is Mom there, too?"

"Of course I am, sweetheart!" Her voice carried faintly through the phone.

"Yes, as you can hear. And Addison?"

"Yeah, Dad?"

"We love you."

"I love you too, Dad."

CHAPTER TWENTY-ONE

GOOD SAMARITAN HOSPITAL. AGAIN.

I saw Mom and Dad standing in the lobby as soon as we got there. They hugged me fiercely. I barely had time to guard my hand.

"You guys look tired," I said once they pulled away. It was true. My dad's shoulders were slumped, and he was in his PJ pants. My mom's hair was puffy in all the wrong places.

"We were in bed watching the game," Dad said, and Mom added, "I nearly died when they showed you two. I thought you were going to go over the edge right along with Devin. I haven't stopped praying since."

Triple-G pulled herself up from the couch and patted my arm. "Every moment a parent prays with worry for her child is a lifetime lived. And believe me, Addison, a few extra generations got tacked onto this family after tonight's stunt."

"Sorry, Triple-G."

"Now don't you go apologizing for saving our little man's life! I'll wring plenty of that out of *him* soon enough!"

"Yes, ma'am," I replied, and she shuffled along to gripe at Devin. He waved her off and looked around.

"Where's Dad and G?" he asked.

"They'll be up in a minute," Triple-G responded. "You know your daddy can't take the stairs."

Since my hand wasn't an emergency, it took a while before someone could see us. I got my cheek kisses from all the Gs, and they helicoptered over my hand and Devin's leg. As we sat in the waiting room, I was perfectly happy to let my parents take care of me. I got a Snickers bar and a cup of hot chocolate, propped up my feet, and watched the TV in the corner.

It shouldn't have, but it shocked me when I saw my own face on the screen.

"Turn it up!" Devin demanded, and Sofia reached to hit the volume button.

"Our top story tonight comes from the Clippers game,

but it has nothing to do with basketball," a newscaster said. He had the thickest mustache I'd ever seen.

"That's right, Greg," the lady anchor continued. "An amazing rescue, caught on camera. It was just after the first quarter that the Staples Center Kiss Cam began its search for some lighthearted action in the crowd."

"And that's where the cameraman found more than he bargained for. Watch as this young man comes flying over the guardrail, and another boy miraculously saves him!"

It was unreal. There was Devin, flipping backward over the guardrail as he tried to slow himself down, and a split second later, I appeared, swiping at his leg and snagging him before he even fell two feet. There was a moment, like time stopped, when I was stretched downward, his leg in my hand, and then I grabbed him with the other hand and both of us were pulled upward, disappearing into the mass of fans and guards who had come to help. The whole thing couldn't have lasted more than four or five seconds. It had felt much, much longer.

The footage shrank into a still image at the corner of the screen—me stretched out as far as I could, Devin dangling spread-eagle below me. It was the same thing I had seen on the jumbotron, burned into my mind. The newscasters kept speaking.

"Arena officials quickly confirmed that both boys are okay. The reason for the fall is still unknown, but Fox 11 News would like to salute the bravery of that boy who risked his own life to save another."

"A very brave young man there, Greg."

I was so stunned that I didn't even realize everyone else in the waiting room had started applauding. Nurses had come out from behind desks. Other people waiting for help were smiling, and some were taking pictures of me on their phones, just like the crowds outside of the emergency station at the arena. I blushed madly, and I tried to hide my face under my jersey. Devin was grinning and bowing to as many people as he could.

That's when it hit me.

I was on film, in photos, and on the news.

Wearing a Blake Griffin jersey.

I didn't even have time to shrug out of it before one of the nurses called, "Addison Gerhardt! You're up!"

The sound of the applause chased us down the hall. We all crammed into the exam room. There was barely enough room for the doctor.

"I hear I've the pleasure of treating a hero this evening," she said as she carefully unwrapped my hand.

"I'm a Warriors fan," I managed after my mom put her hand on my shoulder.

She laughed. "Well, we won't hold that against you here."

The doctor was very patient, and very nice. She politely ushered everyone out when it came time for X-rays, and she let them back in again as she changed my bandages. She didn't even seem to mind as all three Gs offered advice on how to best treat my fingers. Triple-G suggested leeches. She was kidding.

I think.

It turned out there were no fractures in my hands—just the ugly, excruciating fingernail thing. The doctor talked to my parents about how to take care of them. No basketball for a couple of months, at least. There was also this goopy stuff to put on, and to top it all off, a tight gray glove, padded at the fingertips. The doctor took a little pair of scissors and cut off the final two fingers and the thumb of the glove so that my unhurt fingers could poke through.

"It looks like you've got a bionic hand there, Addison!"

We all turned at once to see who had spoken. Devin gasped and ran to his father, who had been wheeled to the exam room by G. He held out his hand to slow his son down, then beckoned him forward for a cautious hug.

"Dad! You're here!" Devin exclaimed. Mrs. Velma seemed less enthusiastic.

"Why on God's green earth are you out of bed?"

"Nurses said it was fine. And besides, if watching my only son throw himself from the top of the Staples Center wasn't enough to give me another heart attack, I think I can handle a drive to the hospital and a couple of hugs."

He got more than a couple. When it was my turn, I had to use my left arm. My right stuck out awkwardly, like I was holding up a peace sign.

"Addison," Mr. Velma said, his hand still on my shoulder. I knelt down in front of him so he wouldn't have to look up. "I'm sure I speak for our entire family when I say that we owe you a debt we cannot repay. Our son is so incredibly lucky to have a friend like you. Were you not by his side, I'm certain he wouldn't be here now. Thank you."

I nodded and offered him a smile. When I stood, I found the rest of the Velma family there, all lined up to thank me. There were five more peace-sign hugs, and all of them repeated what Mr. Velma had said: if I wasn't there, Devin wouldn't be here now.

I knew exactly what they meant, and despite the pain in my hand, I was in total agreement. Still, as I heard their thanks, I couldn't help but start to think of it in another way: If I hadn't agreed to help Devin with his schemes, would we have been at the game at all?

CHAPTER TWENTY-TWO

SOAKING IT ALL IN

I was so exhausted by the time we got home that I fell asleep still wearing the Blake Griffin jersey. My mom and dad both tucked me in, making sure the blanket was rolled away from my hand and that my head hit the pillow. I think they pulled my shoes off for me, too. At least, I woke up barefoot.

The clock above my closet said it was twelve forty-five in the afternoon. I had to rub my eyes twice to read it, and I accidentally smashed my glove-covered fingers into the side of my nose. I gasped. There was nothing quite like pain to get you moving.

I finally tossed the Blake Griffin jersey away and wandered down the hall. I thought about stopping at the bathroom to check my bandages and put some medicine on my fingertips, but the smell coming from the kitchen was too tempting.

"There's the hero of the day!" my mom said. My dad was at the stove, frying up a panful of cinnamon-sugar apples. On the table was a huge waffle and a plate of spicy sausage. Mom pulled out the chair for me. I had two sausage links in my mouth before my backside hit the seat.

"We made your favorites," Dad said. "Twice."

Mom smiled, pointing at the trash can. A cold waffle sat atop a mound of eggshells. Its edges were jagged.

"I may have done some nibbling when it was apparent you weren't going to get out of bed at your normal time."

"Thanks, guys," I said. "For both breakfasts."

"You earned it!" a voice called out from below. "Good morning, Addison!"

"Good afternoon!" I yelled back. "Hi, Ms. Culverson!"

"You need anything else up there? I've got OJ if the kid wants some!"

My dad crouched by the hole. "No thanks, we're good."

"My whole poker crew saw Addison on the eleven o'clock news last night. Your son giving out autographs yet?"

I laughed, holding up my right hand. My mom giggled,

too, and she swiped a strawberry off the side of my plate. Dad hurried back to the apples before they burned, and he brought the whole pan over, tipping the entire sizzling cascade of caramel and apple chunks onto my waffle. After he let the pan rattle into the sink, he returned to the hole.

"No autographing for Addison, I'm afraid. Apparently, it takes quite a bit of effort to catch a kid half your size."

"Dad!" I exclaimed.

"Teasing! We—"

The sound of the phone ringing cut my dad off.

"I've got this one," he said. "You dote on our son."

As Dad answered the phone, Mom leaned in.

"That's maybe, like, the tenth or eleventh call this morning."

"People checking if I'm okay?"

"Some. Moms and dads of your friends at school. A few have been news stations."

It was suddenly hard to swallow the mouthful of apples and waffle I'd been chewing. I took a gulp of milk from the glass nearby and managed to wrangle it down.

"News stations?" I echoed.

"You made quite a scene! We're not surprised. And don't worry," she said, reaching out to cover my good hand with hers. "You don't have to talk to them unless you want to. I think you had enough exposure yesterday. A lot of practice, hmm?"

I thought about the crowd of people outside the emergency station at the stadium, and I shivered.

"Yeah . . ."

"Then you leave the phone calls to us. Maybe try to get your homework done and take it easy today. Eat another dozen waffles."

I smiled. "Deal."

After I finished eating, I retreated to my room. Homework, fortunately, was a bunch of reading and only a little bit of math. It took me a few seconds to work out how to handle the pencil, but once I found that I could hold it like a knife and sort of stab down at the paper, I was fine. I spent most of the rest of the afternoon in there, happy to be hidden away—the phone kept ringing and ringing.

It was near dinnertime, just as I was thinking about scoring another round of waffles, that my mom stuck her head in, the cordless phone in her hand.

"This is one I think you might want to take," she said, smiling. I flopped onto my bed, and she put the phone in my left hand.

"Addi!" Devin said.

"How did you know I had the phone?"

"You always sigh right before you put it up to your ear."

"No, I don't." *Do I?* Okay, I probably did.

"Have you gone on your computer yet, man?"

"No. I woke up way late and have been doing my homework. How's your dad?"

There were a few seconds of silence.

"He's okay," Devin whispered. Then, much louder, "I have twelve thousand followers, Addi! Overnight!"

I palmed my face with my other hand . . . gently.

"That's great, Devin. Your plan worked."

"You should see some of these tweets on my feed. Here. I'll read them to you."

"You don't have to—"

"*Yo Devin! That was scary last night! Glad U . . .* She types out the letter *U* here, by the way. You know, like R-S-T-U, instead of the word *you*—"

"Yeah, I get it, Devin."

"Good. Anyway, *Glad U R okay!*"

"Who's that from?"

"Some girl I don't know. Here's another: *Wow! You're that kid that fell!!!* And the next one: *So happy 2 see U okay! U should thank that guy who caught U!*"

"I'm really happy for you, Devin. Now we—"

"Hold on, bro. I haven't gotten to the best part. Are you ready for this?"

I stared up at the Y-shaped crack in the ceiling. "Yeah, I guess."

"*@ THE game last night. Saw this whole thing. Kid is my new hero! #greatcatch #thecatch #catch #Valentines #miraclekid.*"

"That's a lot of hashtags."

"They're not just any hashtags. They're her hashtags, Addi!"

I flipped the phone to the other hand, regretted it, and flipped it back.

"Her?"

"Jeska Stone's! And she posted a video she caught on her phone! I'm on her Twitter! Well, I mean, you're there, too, of course, but *I'm* on there! Should I message her to tell her who I am? Should I tweet at her? Do you think she'd retweet me?"

"I think she probably doesn't even read her own Twitter feed. She's gotta have people for that, right? Like, servants or something?"

"I think they call them assistants."

"Yeah, those."

"I'm gonna tweet her. Maybe make an Instagram account, too."

"What about your homework?"

"*Pssh.* I think I pretty much have the best excuse of all time. And besides, I might not even be in school tomorrow. I've got to decide which interviews we're going to do."

"Interviews?" I gulped.

"Yeah, man. And don't tell me you haven't been getting offers. I've got a busy signal every time I've called your landline."

"Yeah . . ."

"Listen. I know talking isn't your thing, but if *Mornings with Darcy and Rob* calls, would you please, please, please agree to do the interview with them? They offered an appearance fee if we gave them an exclusive, but they said they'd only do it if they had you, too. *Darcy and Rob*! That's the biggest show in L.A.! And it's syndicated!"

"I know who Darcy and Rob are, Devin."

"Then you'll do it? Appearance fee, man . . ."

I sat up straighter. "Like how much? Enough to cover your dad's bills?"

"Nah. Not even close. But think of the followers I'd pick up!"

"I don't know. . . . There's a whole audience there, right? Like, hundreds of people watching?"

"That's just in-studio, Addi. Millions more watch on TV at home! Think of the exposure we'd get!"

Oh, I was.

Devin kept going. "And Addi? The appearance fee—we *both* get it. Isn't there anything you could use five thousand dollars for?"

I had to shake my head to clear it. Five thousand dollars? I thought of the envelope from the government. I thought of the stupid dishwasher crashing through our floor. I thought of my dad, who'd be home right now if he didn't have to take the taxi back to the garage. Was five thousand dollars enough for a down payment on a new car?

"I'll . . . I'll think about it," I said, and I hung up.

The rest of the day we left the phone disconnected. We still got calls on my mom's cell, but the TV stations didn't have that number, so it was much quieter. I sat back and watched movies while my parents brought me food. I had to admit, it was nice—not that I wanted to make a habit out of scaring them half to death.

In the morning, Dad bit the bullet and drove me to

school in the taxi, since he was worried about reporters. He wasn't wrong, either: there were two news vans outside our apartment building and three more in front of the school. He drove me to the teachers' parking lot and waited for a faculty member to pull up. It turned out to be Coach, who also taught sixth-grade PE.

"Coach Bach!" my dad hollered from the taxi. "Coach!"

Coach hustled up to the window, his track pants swishing with each step. If I was ever going to work at a school, I'd be a gym teacher, for sure. They got to wear the comfortable clothes.

"There he is!" Coach said, reaching through the window to offer me a high five. I held up my glove and shrugged. Coach's face fell.

"The price of heroism," he mumbled. "How long are we going to be without our star player?"

I sighed. "Two months, at least."

"Missing the rest of the season?"

I nodded, and I felt a little queasy. It seemed more real now that Coach knew.

"Well, focus on getting better, and don't worry about disappointing the team. Yes, it's . . ." His voice dropped much lower, and he puffed out his chest. *"Sixth-grade basketball!"*

Then he exhaled and spoke more softly. "But it's also just sixth-grade basketball."

My dad nodded in agreement. "Good point, Coach, and thank you. May I ask you for a favor?"

"Anything, Mr. Gerhardt."

"I believe I spotted some press vans outside the front of the school."

"You surely did. I saw them, too, and Principal Carrillo sent out an e-mail last night warning us. We've got three faculty members out by the wall this morning. Don't worry, Mr. Gerhardt. We'll keep the kids well insulated."

"And we appreciate that. Do you think that you might have time to walk Addison into the building, maybe let him stay in the gym until the bell rings?"

"I think that can be arranged, yes," Coach said, smiling as he scratched his blond beard. He opened the door for me and grabbed my backpack. After I said good-bye to Dad, Coach snuck us around the back way. He let me turn on all the gym lights, which popped satisfyingly as they warmed up. I helped him set up the square plastic scooters for fourth-grade gym class, and he even fed me the ball for five minutes while I shot left-handed jumpers.

"See? Maybe it was a blessing in disguise," Coach joked.

"You'll be ambidextrous by the time you're all healed. You'll have to thank Devin for letting you save him!"

I smiled. Hanging out with Coach made me feel a little better about having to miss the rest of the season, but I'd still suffer without it. Basketball wasn't my favorite sport just because I was tall. It was the pace of the game: everything happened so fast that there wasn't any time to think. And less thinking? That meant less freezing.

The best was when Coach drew up plays. He'd use a dry-erase board to design a backdoor cut off the inbounds, or tweak our 2-3 zone to account for a kid who could shoot from the wing. Everything I needed to do was laid out for me; all I had to do was follow the big letter *A* on the board.

As I stared out at the hallway full of kids, wondering how many of them had seen the game or heard the news, I wished Coach had a play to get me to homeroom. Maybe if I rushed out right when the bell rang, there'd be so many lockers slamming, kids yelling, and backpacks brushing by that I'd be able to sneak through.

Or maybe not.

"Ohh man!" I heard as soon as I stepped into the hallway. The fourth graders had already started lining up to go into the gym, and at the head of the line was Benji. His eyes were as big as golf balls. I tried to ask him what his freckle count was this morning, but he wouldn't even let me talk.

"Addi! Addi! Did you, like, see yourself? It was awesome! Devin was all like, runrunrun, 'n' you were all like, 'Noooo! Wait, bro!' and he was all like, 'Aaaah!' and you were all like, 'I've got you, bro!' and then it was the falling and the snagging and the cheering and . . . Addi!"

You wouldn't think someone could successfully reenact my catch of Devin, especially not a fourth grader (by himself, in a crowded hallway, on the linoleum floor), but he pulled it off. Sort of. It was mostly just Benji rolling around, grabbing his own ankle, doing some sort of handstand thing, and then collapsing in a heap and panting. I helped him up with my left hand, and all the other fourth graders murmured, "Oooh."

"I touched him!" Benji exclaimed, and he held his hand out so that the other little kids could feel his fingers. I rolled my eyes, but it was hard not to smile as I left them and headed toward homeroom.

When I got to the classroom, Devin was already there. He was standing on a desktop, his arms out wide, with fifteen other kids gathered around him. Even Ms. Gillespie was watching . . . and seemed fine with him being up there.

"And then the world turned upside down! I felt completely weightless, completely free. It was like I was an eagle, soaring on the roars of the crowd." He paused, pointed at Ms. Gillespie, and snapped his fingers. "That was a simile I just threw in there for you, ma'am." She nodded, and he continued. "And then, out of absolutely nowhere, divine intervention!"

"Addi!" Martina Ruiz shouted, her curly hair bouncing as she sprinted over and gave me a hug. Two seconds later and I was mobbed.

Devin extended both hands toward me and said, "Right on cue. Nobody can say the guy doesn't have impeccable timing!"

Holding my own sore hand above the crowd and whispering a prayer of thanks for being the tallest kid in the grade, I waded through the kids to my desk and sat down. I looked at Ms. Gillespie, but she winked, then pointed at the clock. There were still five minutes left in homeroom.

"Enjoy it," she mouthed. I shivered.

Devin, I thought, was enjoying it enough for the both of us.

CHAPTER TWENTY-THREE

SQUEEZING IT ALL OUT

So it turned out my dad couldn't pick me up from school until after his shift was over at five o'clock. Normally that wasn't an issue, but since I couldn't go to basketball practice, that left me with two hours to kill. I would have loved to have gone across the street to grab a snack at the food trucks, then maybe hung out at the park with some of the other guys, but that was a no-go, too. Principal Carrillo made the call: she didn't want Devin or me out there by ourselves, not with the press still hanging around. And boy, were they still hanging around. We could see their trucks—five of them now—from the windows of the detention room.

"Five trucks? That's it?" Devin moaned. He had to wait

for Sofia to pick him up, so he was stuck like me. We weren't *in* detention, but it was the only place that had a teacher who could supervise us.

"You wanted more?" Gage whispered. He *was* in detention.

"I just thought, you know, with forty-three thousand followers on Twitter, the media might want a bigger piece of me," Devin said, tossing his shoulders back and shooting a sly grin at me.

"Forty-three thousand?" Gage said. "Nuh-uh."

Devin smiled. Gage had taken the bait.

"Check it out."

Devin rummaged in his backpack, then took out his phone. The detention monitor had stepped out into the hallway to speak with an angry parent—probably Gage's mom—and had closed the door behind her so we couldn't hear their argument. That was a two-way street, of course. . . .

"Oh," Devin said, slumping. "I was wrong."

Gage smirked but it didn't last long.

"Yeah," Devin crowed. "Did I say forty-three thousand? I meant sixty-three. Must have picked up twenty thousand more since this morning."

"'Grats, dude," Gage said after a bit. "But all you did was fall. If Addison had a Twitter account, I'd bet he—"

"He does!" Devin said, laughing. "I made him one so he'd be my first follower. Hold on, I'll sign in for him!"

"Don't," I murmured, blushing.

"No worries, Addi. I'm sure you're not going to ha—"

It was Devin who froze for a change.

"What? Lemme see!" Gage whined, and he craned over to see the phone screen.

"I, uh . . . I don't . . . ," Devin mumbled.

"Holy crap! Is that millions, like in *millions*?"

I gasped, and I scrambled to peek at what they saw.

There was my terrible school picture, my name, and my number of followers.

"I have . . . two million followers?"

"Two-point-six," Gage whispered. "That's, like, more than Billy Crystal!"

Devin shot him a look. My lips started trembling, and I had to sit down again.

"Delete it," I said after a moment.

"How did you get more followers than me?" Devin asked, scowling.

"I don't care. Delete it."

"I mean, you don't post. You didn't tell ESPN your name!

How did people even find you, unless . . ." He trailed off, typing and swiping furiously at his screen. "No way. She followed you?"

"*She?*"

"Jeska Stone! And now her followers are following you! How did she even . . . unless . . . unless she searched my page, then looked at who followed me . . ."

"Heh," Gage snickered, "they just, like, used you as a bathroom break on their way to Addison."

Devin huffed, and he started to put his phone away. Then, though, he whipped it back out.

"This isn't fair," he grumbled. "No way you should have more followers than me. No way."

I put my good hand on his arm. He shrugged me off.

"If you delete my account, I won't have any followers."

He started typing again, and I thought he was taking my advice. Instead, though, he declared, "There. I just tweeted from your account, *THX 4 following me! U should check @ LilSwaggyD47 4 more news. <3 ADDI.*"

"Seriously?" I sighed.

"What do you care? It's not like you check it, or do anything with it."

"But it's me! That's my picture, and my name, and maybe I don't want everyone in the world to be able to see that!" I shouted. A wave of heat prickled up my neck and into my cheeks. After a couple seconds, it settled right behind my eyes, and I could feel it wriggling around back there, trying to escape as tears. I grabbed my backpack, shut my eyes, and stumbled my way out of the classroom. The detention monitor stopped mid-sentence to call after me, but I was stomping down the hall too fast, and Gage's mom was still wagging her finger in the monitor's face.

Flap, flap, flap went my beat-up old shoe, all the way out the front doors of the school, all the way to the wall. I'd walk home if I had to.

Or not.

"That's the kid!" a man exclaimed, and he snapped his fingers at another guy in the back of a van. The second man hoisted a big camera onto his shoulder, and they jogged toward me before I even made it to the sidewalk. Four more pairs just like them fought over one another to get to me. I spun on my heel as fast as I could, and I nearly tripped as the bottom of my shoe disintegrated. I left the cruddy old piece of rubber sitting there, my sock peeking out as I ran back into the building.

I paused to catch my breath, and I dared to look over my shoulder through the glass doors. It was like there was something magical about that short sandstone wall. All five news crews had stopped at the gate, set up, and started filming. I guess they had been waiting for something to happen, and it didn't much matter what.

I suppose I shouldn't have been surprised when, after one of the crews finished, a well-dressed lady with a microphone looked around, brushed her hair from her face, and crept in to grab the piece of my shoe I had left behind. I looked down at my foot, a drop of sweat dripping off my nose and tapping the worn-out toe. Reluctantly, I undid the laces, slipped the shoe off, and set it gently in the nearby trash can.

I had really liked that pair of shoes.

As I trudged my way back toward the detention room, I heard familiar voices. I peeked around the corner to see Sofia. Gage's mom was gone, and Devin was standing next to his sister, his face illuminated by the screen of his phone. It let me see the glint of tears on his cheeks. I thought about going up to apologize for screaming at him, but I couldn't get my feet to move—especially not the shoeless one. I told myself it was because I was too embarrassed to have Sofia see me that way, because of course I wanted to tell Devin I was sorry.

Didn't I?

When they were gone, I slipped into the room to wait for

my dad. The detention monitor tried to get me to tell her what had happened, but my throat wasn't working so well, and she dropped it after a few minutes. We waited the rest of the hour in silence, her doing some grading, and me contemplating my sock.

When my dad strolled into the room and saw me, he smiled softly. "One shoe gone, eh? My boy, you either had the most incredible day of school ever, or the roughest."

I shrugged.

"Bit of both?"

I nodded.

He got my backpack for me, then reached down to help me up. I couldn't remember the last time I'd held his hand, but I didn't feel like pulling away, not even as we made our way out to the teachers' lot.

My dad didn't say anything until we were almost home.

"So, what's your guess, Addison?"

"Guess?" I asked quietly.

"Yeah. We plugged the phone back in this morning. How many calls, you think? Our voice mail has enough memory for about an hour of messages. Think they took it all?"

I thought of the scrambling news teams. "Probably."

"You don't have to listen to them if you don't want. A lot of them are likely to be well-wishers, though—friends and such. If you're up for it, we'd like you to hear at least a few. Some people have been very kind, and I think they might cheer you up."

"Okay," I said.

Dad dropped me off right at the curb, and my mom was there waiting to bring me upstairs. He had to take the taxi back to the garage, then take the bus home. There were a few news vans outside our apartment, but they couldn't get their act in gear before we snuck inside.

"How was your day?" my mom asked, wrapping her arm around my shoulders as we went upstairs. She had to climb a step ahead of me to manage the height difference, but she did, the whole way.

"It wasn't great," I admitted. "Lost my shoe."

"So I saw. I think your brother has a spare pair of loafers in his closet that might fit you. Not what you're used to, I know, but they'll do until we can go get you another pair."

"When will that be?"

"I don't know, honey. Might be a bit—at least, until we

can leave the apartment without being mobbed. Maybe a couple of days? I'm sure this will all die down when they realize we're not saying much."

I kicked off my other shoe when we made it inside. I thought about throwing it away, too, but decided to tuck it under my bed instead. It had done its job well, after all, and had just lost its companion. I felt bad for it.

When I went into the kitchen, my mom was already washing the lettuce for a salad. The phone light was blinking, which meant the voice mail was full.

"Dad was right. So many messages today."

"Did he ask you about listening to a few?"

"Yeah."

"Go for it. Feel free to just skip the ones from the news places."

"Can I take the phone into my room?"

"Sure. Dinner will be ready in about ten minutes."

I wasn't cold, but I pushed my feet under my blanket after I collapsed into bed. I dialed the number for voice mail and skipped the message warning me that it was full.

"Addison!" the first message said. "This is Grandma Velma. We're all thinking of you, and hope you slept well."

In the background, I could hear Double-G and Triple-G squabbling about something. I smiled.

The second, third, and fourth messages were all from TV stations. I deleted them without listening.

The fifth message was an automatic note from our landlord's office, reminding us that rent was due at the end of the month. I rolled my eyes and deleted that one, too.

Message six started off just like the other TV station ones. Before I could hit the delete button, though, a cheerful woman's voice said, "That's right, Addison! We here at *Mornings with Darcy and Rob* would love to bring you on the show for an interview, because we believe in honoring hometown heroes, accidental or otherwise. As our previous messages have mentioned, we'd like to show our appreciation for your heroic actions by offering a substantial appearance stipend, in return for an exclusive interview. If that sounds interesting to you, please do call our booking manager, Stephanie Morrison, at 213-555-0199."

She repeated the number a few more times, and on the last one, I paused the message. I considered writing the number down, but remembered my achy fingers, so instead I just gritted my teeth and dialed. As it rang, I thought about Devin. He'd be a natural up on that stage. Totally fearless.

"*Darcy and Rob*, this is Stephanie speaking. How may I help you?"

"Um." I closed my eyes. Like that would help—I was alone in my own bedroom.

"Is someone there?" Stephanie asked. She sounded very friendly.

"Addison Gerhardt," I mumbled.

"Oh, hey! You're him! Wow! We were so hoping you'd call! Honestly, we were expecting your parents to communicate with us, but I'm not surprised, frankly. I should've known you would handle this from what we saw during the game!"

Say thank you.

NOPE.

Say you understand.

NOPE.

Hang up!

NOPE.

I let the phone drop into my lap, still cradled in my good hand. I felt sick. I probably would have been sick, too, if my mom hadn't come to check on me.

"Are you talking to someone, Addison?"

It took me a couple of moments to thaw, but having Mom there always helped.

"Yes, Mom. It's *Mornings with Darcy and Rob*. This is Stephanie. They want me to come on and do an interview."

My mom sat down next to me, one hand on my knee. The other she used to pry the phone from my grip. She put it on speaker.

"This is Addison's mother, Anna Gerhardt."

"Oh, perfect! We'd love to have Addison in for a couple segments of our show! They run about five minutes, simple Q and A, then some photos with Darcy and Rob during the commercial break. He'll be in and out of the studio in an hour, and that includes hair and makeup."

"I see," my mom replied.

"Also, I'd be remiss if I didn't mention the stipend. We think it's more than competitive, but we do ask for an exclusive. I hope that's not a problem."

My mom looked at me, and I shrugged. Stephanie jumped into the silence.

"Of course, since Addison is a minor, Mrs. Gerhardt, you'll have to accept the check on his behalf. Again, I think you'll find it above and beyond the industry norm, even for other nationally syndicated shows. *The Ellen DeGeneres Show*, for example—"

"Can you hold on for just a second, Stephanie?" my mom asked.

"Absolutely!"

Mom squeezed my knee, then covered the phone with her hand. "Do you want to do an interview, sweetie? This would be a huge step for you. . . ."

I closed my eyes and exhaled slowly.

"C—can I think about it?"

Mom uncovered the phone.

"When do you need a decision, Stephanie?"

"Well, that's the thing. This is a time-sensitive offer. That's how news works, unfortunately. Have you ever heard the phrase 'fifteen minutes of fame'? It's like that. The further away we get from the event, the less impactful it is for viewers. I know it sounds terrible, but that's the business. We're looking to get you on the show in the next couple of days—maybe Wednesday or Thursday at the latest."

I had started to sweat, and my fingers were burning.

"Addison?" my mom said gently. "It's up to you, baby. Do you want to do the interview?"

Devin's dad. That stupid dishwasher. Uber.

Devin's dad . . .

I opened my eyes and looked down at my feet. The blanket had come off, and I could see my socks.

"Yeah," I sighed. "I guess I do."

CHAPTER TWENTY-FOUR

THE RIGHT HOOK OF DEVIN VELMA

My brother's loafers barely fit, and there was no way they matched my basketball shorts or my Klay Thompson jersey. Still, it was better than going to school barefoot.

But not much.

At least I wasn't too worried about it. No, that part of my brain was pretty well occupied with stressing about the interview and looking for Devin. I found him in homeroom again, but he wasn't standing on top of any desks this time. Instead, he had his head down on one, a Dodgers hat pulled low to cover up his face.

I slipped into the seat next to him and glanced at Ms. Gillespie. She gave me a little nod, so I leaned in to whisper to him.

"Devin? Are you okay? I'm sorry about . . ."

I trailed off as he lifted a little, sliding a small packet of papers along the desk without taking his head off his arm. I picked them up and looked. They were black-and-white copies of that image of me at the arena, stretching down and catching Devin.

Or what should've been Devin.

In each one, Devin was cut out and replaced by other things. The first made it look like I was catching a giant kitten, its sad little eyes facing the camera. Beneath it were the words "Hang in there!" The second had replaced Devin with a football, and the caption said "Immaculate Reception, Part Two." Whoever made it had even changed the picture to make it look like I was wearing a San Francisco 49ers jersey. I winced. That wasn't any better than Blake Griffin.

"Are they all—"

"Keep looking," Devin mumbled into his sleeve.

I did. There was one of me catching the president of the United States, another with a turkey leg in my hand and a huge shark jumping at it, and one that looked like some painting, my fingers reaching out and almost touching the hand of an old guy with a white beard.

"Where did you get these?"

"The internet. I printed them off this morning."

"Are you mad about them? Don't worry. They don't hurt my feelings. I mean, sure, they're pretty dumb; I don't think I could really catch the president. He's heavier than you, for sure, and—"

"I'm mad because I'm not in them, Addison!"

He sat up, and I could see that his eyes were red. His nose was, too. I held up a hand to assure Ms. Gillespie that I had it under control.

Only, I didn't.

"It's okay, Devin."

"It's not okay!" Devin yelled. The rest of the kids in the classroom went completely silent. They knew when a kid was revving up to put on a show, and as far as they were concerned, Devin was kicking it into high gear.

"They're just pictures," I offered, blushing.

"Of you! Everyone wants to follow you! It was supposed to be me getting famous, me breaking the Curse, and instead it's all about you!"

Ms. Gillespie stood up. "Devin, maybe we should take a walk out into the hall?"

He slipped out of his desk like he was going with her, but then turned on me.

"Why don't you get it? Why can't you see what you're doing to me?"

"Why don't *you* get it?" I spat back, and I jumped to my feet. "I don't want any of this. You made that Twitter account for me. You wanted to go to the game. You wanted to do the interview with Darcy and Rob! Well, guess what? You don't get to drag me around anymore! As soon as I get home, I'm calling Stephanie and telling her I'm not going!"

"What?" Devin said, suddenly quiet. Ms. Gillespie gently tugged at his shoulder. He pushed her hand off.

"You heard me! I'm not going, because this has gone too far. I should have refused to get those tickets. I never should have let you go to the game. I should have told you how stupid you were as soon as you said you were doing the Backflip of Doom!"

I wish I had frozen then. Why didn't I freeze? All those eyes on me, I should have frozen. But I was so angry, and so tired, and it felt so good to unload. It made my fingers hurt less and the image of my dad yelling at the envelope go away and the guilt over riding in the Uber disappear. I should have been able to taste the hatefulness I was about to spew, maybe slap those fingers over my mouth—anything to keep from saying what I did.

But I was on a roll, and there wasn't a NOPE in sight.

"That's all your 'Curse' is! Just you looking for attention like always! Hell, you were probably jealous that your dad had a heart attack, because it meant your family wasn't watching *The Devin Show* for two whole weeks! So there you go, looking for idiotic ways to get your followers, and your views, and you couldn't stop. In fact, I bet you never really cared about saving your dad at all!"

The class gasped. Ms. Gillespie wrung her hands. Devin stood there, shaking.

And then he punched me in the face.

CHAPTER TWENTY-FIVE

MOTHER KNOWS BEST

My mom was a teacher. She got up every day, put her grading into her bag, took the bus to school, and set up her classroom. She had curriculum meetings and a dry-erase board and her own parking spot that she never used.

Yes, she worked as a teacher.

But she was really a fighter, and there was nobody she fought harder for than me. I learned that early on. First grade, in fact.

The Garbageman Fiasco was something I didn't like to talk about, but it was a good example of what my mom was capable of. I was in Ms. Abernathy's class. She was what my mom called "old guard." Taught the same lesson plans for thirty years. Still used a chalkboard. Did her grades in an actual book. And every year, she led her students in the Letterville Parade.

Okay, so it wasn't so much a parade as a line, but there was no way Ms. Abernathy was changing the name or how it worked. Each kid was given a job in the magical land of Letterville, based on the first letter of his or her last name. It would have been fine if we got to pick, but we didn't: the jobs were part of an old kit she had, complete with costume ideas and a script for the kid to say. Devin was a veterinarian. Marielle Brown was a banker.

Addison Gerhardt?

Garbageman.

When I got the card with my job, my script, and my costume idea, I didn't think much of it. Sure, it seemed a little weird that the costume would be a trash bag with holes cut out and pieces of garbage stapled to it, but I was an Oscar the Grouch fan anyway, and I thought Devin's outfit, which featured tons of stuffed animals sitting on his shoulders and arms, was even worse.

I was wrong.

I went to my mom's room after school that day, just like I always did, and I showed her my card. Her nostrils got big. Her eyebrows shot up. Her jaw got really tight. And then she grabbed my arm, and we marched down the hall to Ms. Abernathy's room.

"My son is not going to be a garbageman."

Ms. Abernathy was cleaning out the guinea pig cage with a paper towel. She paused, letting the paper towel go. It fluttered down, where Miss Squeakers snagged it and commenced nibbling. Slowly, Ms. Abernathy turned to face my mom.

"And why not, Mrs. Gerhardt?"

"It's ridiculous. He'll be teased for years!"

I shrank back, thinking this sounded like the kind of conversation I should probably wait in the hallway for. My mom wouldn't let go of my wrist, though.

"Teased? Whatever for?"

I was curious, too. It didn't seem that bad to me.

At least, not yet.

"First off, the costume. Wearing trash? His friends will laugh at him up on that stage. The whole school will. And second, *garbageman*? It's *sanitation worker*, if anything!"

Ms. Abernathy took a deep breath, then lit into my mom. "I think you're being too politically correct. I've been at this for decades, and not a child or parent has complained. Your oversensitivity is doing that boy more harm than good!"

My mom's grip on my wrist tightened. I can remember it actually hurting. Then she looked down at me, her nostrils even bigger, eyebrows even higher, and jaw even stonier.

"Addison, baby. Wait out in the hall for me."

I'd never run so fast in my life. And even though I was out of the room, I could still hear them arguing. The louder they got, the smaller I felt. I wasn't even sure what they were saying, but by the time they were done, I knew one thing for sure.

There was no way I wanted to be a garbageman.

In the end, I think my mom won. At least, I remember her working on a costume the next week, and it didn't involve trash. There was a bow tie, a blazer, an American flag sticker, and a "Vote for Addison!" sign, but no garbage. I never got to wear it, though, because on the day that the Letterville Parade rolled around, I felt so sick that I couldn't go in to school. My mom said that was just fine by her. She stayed home with me, and we watched cartoons for hours.

So yeah, my mom was a fighter. And that came with certain advantages.

But there were disadvantages, too. The one that I feared most was the complete and total inability to just skate by her. Every single thing I did, I had to own. So after school on the day Devin punched me, I was forced to wait, slouched over in Dad's leather chair, while she spoke on the phone with Mrs. Velma. The whole time, she stood in the doorway of the living room, leaned up against the frame, staring at me. She never said more than "Mm-hmm," or "I see" until the very end, when she slipped back into the kitchen and I couldn't hear her anymore.

I poked at my face gently. It felt like someone had pressed a doughnut around my left eye and told me to look through the hole. At least it was a little open now. Back at school, it had swollen up so bad I couldn't see out of it at all.

When my mom returned, she had an ice pack in her hand instead of the phone. She handed it to me, then pulled over the footstool and sat down. I covered up my eye and tried to look pathetic.

It didn't work.

"So, Devin is suspended for the rest of the week. His parents are furious with him, but he's not talking. They apologize on his behalf."

I nodded. It made my head throb.

Mom lifted her hand, pressing it softly to the ice pack to help me hold it there. I covered her hand with mine. It was warm against the cold.

"My baby's first black eye," she said, smiling. "I'm sorry this happened to you. Tough week, hmm?"

"Yeah. Really tough."

"I know, baby, and we're here for you," she cooed. But then she grew quiet, and her smile faded. "I do have one *tiny* question, though, if you feel up for answering it."

It would've been nice to cover up both eyes with the ice pack right about then, but she was having none of it.

"Okay," I mumbled.

"Thanks, Addison. Here's the scenario: I've got two boys, best friends since forever. Amazingly, miraculously, one of them saves the other's life. Then, two days later, one is punching the other in the face in the middle of homeroom, with the teacher right there. Now, I feel terribly for the boy who got punched. Who wouldn't? Especially since he's my baby. But, Addison, sweetie, I've got to ask myself, and I've got to ask you . . . what could one of those boys have said that would be so bad as to make the other punch him in the face?"

And so I told her—not just about what I'd said to Devin, but about all of it. I started from the beginning with the Backflip of Doom, through the Kiss Cam plan, all the way to the hairball of hate I'd coughed up in homeroom.

CHAPTER TWENTY-SIX

EPIPHANY: NOUN: A SUDDEN REALIZATION

While I was busy staring at a blank piece of paper, my mom was on the phone. She was just hanging up when I poked my head into the kitchen.

"That was Stephanie over at *Mornings with Darcy and Rob*, calling about the interview tomorrow morning," she said. It was tough to tell from her voice whether she was still in yell-at-me mode. "They were disappointed to hear that Devin wouldn't be able to make it."

A wave of guilt washed over me. "His parents . . ."

"Told him he can't go. He's being punished, just like you."

I took a deep breath. To tell the truth, I was relieved when I told Devin I was backing out—no answering questions, no scary crowds, no pressure.

That was another thing about having a fighter for a mom . . . most parents would freak out, maybe send me to my room until I was willing to "tell the truth," or just laugh in my face and call back Mrs. Velma to ask if this was some elaborate prank. Not my mom, though. She didn't take her eyes off me the entire time, and when I was done, she nodded and said, "That seems about right."

I looked down at my legs, then at the arm of the chair, then at her, then back down at my legs, waiting for her to say something else, but she was silent.

It was more uncomfortable than my eye and fingers combined.

"So . . . ," I finally offered.

"So here's what's going to happen," she said suddenly, shooting up from the stool. The ice pack fell into my lap. I didn't have the courage to pick it up.

"Yes, this is the plan," she continued, pacing back and forth and waving her finger in the air. "Devin isn't talking to anyone, so my son can't call him and apologize. Devin is suspended, so my son can't find him at school tomorrow. But my son will apologize. Oh, yes, he will."

The way she said *my son* was terrifying—equal parts fiercely possessive and intensely disappointed. I pulled my knees up to my chest and hugged them, ice pack stinging my belly.

"And because my son *needs* to apologize, he will march into his room immediately. My son will sit down at his desk, take a piece of paper, and he will write a note to his best friend Devin."

I held up my injured hand, but she scowled at me and waved that finger.

"Eh, eh, eh! He will write the note with the pen in his teeth if he must! In that note, my son will explain himself, and will express his remorse for saying such hateful, hurtful things. And then my son will carry that note on his person every waking moment of every day, until he sees his best friend Devin again, and he gives it to him. When that day arrives, my son will no longer be grounded. He will be able to play basketball again, and go out to movies again, and visit places other than school, the library, or home. Assuming the apology is accepted, he may be able to watch TV or play video games again. Do I make myself clear, *my son?*"

My mouth was open. My legs slid downward, and when my feet hit the floor, the ice pack slipped off the chair and landed with a splat. I didn't dare pick it up. With her dark eyes burning into my back, I marched into my room.

I sat down at my desk.

I took out a piece of paper.

And I stared at it.

Usually, I was better on paper than I was out loud; the only way I had survived all the book reports in fourth grade was that I was able to stand there and read from the sheet, pretending that no one else was around. But here I was, alone, and I was frozen as badly as if I had been up on a stage, wearing a garbage bag and listening to the entire school laugh at me. I tried to think of what to say to Devin that would make up for telling him he was just trying to hog the attention away from his sick dad, but no matter how hard I slapped the side of my head or how wide-eyed I stared at the paper, I couldn't come up with anything. Heck, I didn't even have a clue what Devin was thinking. When had this become about which one of us had more followers, or who was pictured on the internet rescuing kittens?

After two hours, I gave up, certain that I wasn't going to be able to apologize. Certain that I didn't deserve a best friend. Certain that I didn't deserve to leave the room anyway. Not if I wasn't able to figure out what was really going on with Devin.

It turned out, though, my mom knew all about that, too.

Then, though, I looked over at the hole in our kitchen floor, and I remembered the money. I hung my head.

"Sorry, Mom. I know I messed the show up, too. I was nervous about it, but I thought that the money could help— pay that water fine, take care of the rent, maybe even let Dad get a car so he could quit the taxi company and work for Uber."

My mom pointed at me with a wooden spoon from the counter. "Three things. First, you're going on that TV show. Your father is taking you, and you're missing the first half of school tomorrow. You made a commitment. Being grounded doesn't save you, and Stephanie said they'd be happy to welcome you on alone. Second, this is a major step for you, and one your father and I think it's time you took. And third, that money is going straight into your college savings account."

"But—"

"But nothing!" said my dad, who had just gotten home. He set his bag down on the kitchen table, took off his hat, and moved over to slip his arm around Mom's waist. He kissed her on the temple and took the spoon, waving it so hard as he talked that he nearly hit the refrigerator. "I love that you're thinking of me, Addison, and of this family, but trust me when I say I'd happily drive that taxi for the rest of my life if you could assure me that when I got home, I'd be able to look above my mantel and see my sons' framed college diplomas."

"Copies of them," my mom joked. "We don't want you living here forever."

"Good point, honey. Copies," Dad confirmed, and he shoved the spoon into the pot of chili thawing over the stove.

"That's not . . . I . . . I can't do it without Devin. . . ."

My mom came around, putting her hands on my shoulders.

"You can, and you will, because it's time. And besides, it's Devin who never could have done it without you."

My eyes widened.

"Wh . . . what?"

"That boy loves attention, Addison. It's what keeps him going. But nobody's attention is more important to him than yours! Why do you think he always waited until you were watching to do those silly dives into the swimming pool every summer?"

My dad laughed. "Or dragged you to his soccer tryouts?"

Mom rolled her eyes. "And don't get us started on the Velma Basement Karaoke Championships . . . Every time: 'Addi! Come down here and listen to me do *The Lion King* again!' Devin has never been able to do anything without his trusty Addison."

Suddenly, I saw it all: Devin grabbing me before the Backflip. Begging me to go to the game. The fifth-grade talent show. Lady Macbeth.

Asking me to be his first follower . . .

"Man . . . ," I murmured. "I'm such an idiot."

My mom sighed. "It hurt him when you told him you wouldn't support him. You made a mistake. But don't beat yourself up too—"

I held up my gloved hand, closed my eyes for a second, and thought.

Then I dashed back to my room.

The words I couldn't find before seemed to fly out of the pencil now. When I was finished, my left hand ached even worse than my right. I had used both sides of the sheet, and my awkward handwriting looked like the jagged lines beeped out by Mr. Velma's heart monitor. Carefully, I folded it up until it was a little triangle, just like the ones we made to play paper football in the cafeteria when it rained. Then I slipped it into my pocket. As soon as I did, though, I heard my mom's voice in my head. *My son will carry that note on his person every waking moment of every day . . .*

My pocket was no good. I wouldn't wear the same pants

to school every day, and what if they got thrown in the wash? I looked for my backpack, but it was out in the hall, and I wasn't ready to face my mom yet. I thought about hole-punching it and wearing it around my neck like a pendant, but that was just weird.

So I did the only other thing I could think of.

I shoved it in my shoe.

If I thought the loafers were tight before, well, there was no way I was forgetting that the note was in there. As I tried the fit, I actually felt better, too. I had said horrible things to my best friend, but the fix, hopefully, was right there, like I had packed my guilt into that little triangle and told it to chill there until it was time for it to go away.

It almost made me think that was my mom's plan in the first place.

CHAPTER TWENTY-SEVEN

MORNINGS WITH DARCY AND ROB

When I told them I had finished the note, my parents welcomed me to the dinner table. As we ate, we talked about what to expect from the talk show the next day—no way was I going into that big of an exposure without a game plan. Unfortunately, none of us was normally home when *Darcy and Rob* was on, so we had to watch as much as we could online, chairs turned toward our old, slow computer as it buffered through an episode.

At least we knew who they were: Darcy was a former Miss California, and she had also gone to the Olympics for synchronized swimming, though we couldn't remember if she had won anything. She was known for being bright, bubbly, and the most fashionable lady on TV. Rob was a former DJ for a big radio show, and he had been on MTV for a while. He was the goofball, always playing pranks and asking dumb questions. In the episode we watched, they were cooking something with a celebrity chef, and every time Darcy turned to talk to the guest, Rob would shake a little bottle of hot sauce over her pan. At the last minute, when it was Rob's turn to ask the chef a question, Darcy switched the pans. Rob ate it, and he went nuts.

Dad said, "These people seriously have the number one talk show in the state?"

My mom nodded. "One of the top shows in the country, in fact."

He shrugged, then took another bite of corn cake.

When dinner was finished, I decided to go to bed early. As I lay there, I regretted it. My mind started playing through all the questions they might ask me, all the jokes they might play on me. I started to fall asleep at one point, but the first dream I had was about Darcy and Rob. In it, they had one of those fifty-foot-tall ladders with a diving board on top. Below was a little bucket of water. Rob was wearing a rainbow pair of swim trunks, flippers, and a yellow duckie inner tube around his belly, just like Devin had when we were little. He was bouncing on the end of the diving board and waving at the screaming, laughing audience. Then the announcer came on and said that it was my job to run out onto the diving board and catch him before he plummeted to his death on live TV.

I woke up sweating just as he started his cannonball.

All told, I probably got an hour of real sleep. Fortunately, when I looked in the mirror in the morning, I didn't seem to have dark circles under my eyes or anything.

No, the raging purple-and-green black eye covered those right up.

I got dressed—nice collared shirt, khakis, white socks, my brother's loafers—and made my way out to breakfast. I was already feeling a bit queasy, so I didn't eat much. Dad sat with me and went over the schedule.

"We get there at nine o'clock; I have a buddy from the company picking us up at eight thirty so we can avoid the buses and people out on the street. He'll pull us right into the studio lot, and Stephanie Morrison should be there to walk us in. Then you go get all fancy with makeup and such—maybe they can do something about that eye—and you're on at nine forty-two. Hmmm. That's precise."

"Do I get, like, a rehearsal or something?"

"Your mother asked. They said no—if it's rehearsed, the

audience can tell, and it seems less authentic. I guess they want it to feel like you're just dropping by on your way to school."

"Do I really have to go to school afterward?"

My dad folded the schedule and put it into his pocket. "You have to ask?"

"I'll grab my backpack," I muttered.

Stephanie might have been right with her fading fifteen minutes theory; as we hustled down to meet Dad's friend, there was only one news van parked outside, and I didn't even see anyone around it. I felt a little better then, like maybe after *Mornings with Darcy and Rob* everything would just go back to normal—at least, as normal as it could be after you taunt your best friend into knuckle-knocking your eye socket.

My dad and his buddy chatted about company stuff for the whole ride. I sat quietly in the back, watching the people on the sidewalks. Every so often, one of them would glance up, and it felt like they were staring at me right through the tinted window. When they did, I'd look away, even though I knew they couldn't really see me.

Unfortunately, when we got to the studio lot, there were no tinted windows to hide behind, and I didn't own a pair of sunglasses. Stephanie saw us from across the way and scampered over, smiling and waving. She stopped both when she got a look at my eye.

"Ew! Oh, er, I mean, oh! That's a . . . well . . . I suppose that explains why Devin won't be joining us this morning. His mother mentioned something about it on the phone, but . . . well . . . yes . . . ," she said. She *was* wearing sunglasses, and she slid them down to peer at my face. She bit her lower lip—she used a lot of shiny pink lip gloss—and then forced herself to smile again. "I guess hair and makeup have their work cut out for them this morning! We'd better get started right away!"

She led my dad and me through a big set of metal doors into a wide concrete hallway. It was much darker than the parking lot, and it took a while for my eyes to adjust. Still, I could see that the hall was lined with all kinds of things: stacks of wood; huge, black-painted banks of lights; tables stacked top to top; and long ladders. It made me think of my dream, and I shuddered.

"The dressing rooms are back this way, through the soundstage," Stephanie said. "Ready to see our set?"

There was a curtain over the entrance, and a man dressed in all black swept it to the side for us. He had a headset on, and the wires dangling from it connected to multiple little boxes on his belt. Beyond the curtain, there were a dozen more men and women dressed the same, all scurrying along. They were moving things, pushing stuff, climbing around, and constantly talking, though it was impossible to tell if they were speaking to the person in front of them or someone in their mics.

It was easy to see why there were so many stage crew members. The room was huge. On one side was a big section of risers, kind of like the ones in the gym at school, only these were padded and looked more comfortable. The risers sat on a round platform, and to my surprise, they started to rotate. I realized it was so the audience could see the different sections of the *Darcy and Rob* set, which was to the right.

If giants were given a fancy house to dissect in science class, the result might have been something like what I saw. There was a bright, cheerful-looking living room with a little table in the middle. A vase of fresh flowers sat on the table. To one side of the table was a couch, lots of pillows piled along the seat. On the other side were two chairs, one white and one brown. Plenty of light streamed in through windows on the side and from a chandelier above the table, and a colorful circular carpet rested on the floor in front of the furniture. Or, it would've been a circular carpet if it hadn't been sliced right down the middle. There was no proper ceiling, either; the chandelier hung from a complicated nest of pipes, wires, and other lights that seemed to go on up into the blackness forever. The light from the window was the result of a huge spotlight behind a blue-tinted sheet. The closer I looked, the less like sunlight it seemed.

Next to the carved-up living room was a half kitchen. There was a refrigerator, a stove, a microwave, and all sorts of machines on the countertops. As we walked by, I realized none of them were plugged in. It was all fake.

It still might have been better than a huge hole in the kitchen floor, though.

"Here we are!" said Stephanie when we had made it past the set. She ushered me into a little room, where two younger women guided me to a chair. The desk nearby had a big mirror, and it was surrounded by bare lightbulbs.

"This is Vic and Casey. They'll know just what to do about that eye. Any questions before I go?"

My dad confirmed the time I'd go on and asked if we'd get to meet Darcy and Rob before the show started.

"Hmm," she said as she thought, and she took out her phone to check the time. "Afraid not. Normally I'd say yes, but with that shiner, Addison's going to need a lot more chair time. Don't worry, though. They're super-friendly, and I'm sure he'll do absolutely fine. They know he's a kid. They're not going to interrogate him or anything. Just some easy questions. All he's really got to do is smile and be chatty. You can handle that, right, Addison?"

Agree.

NOPE.

Nod.

NOPE.

My dad put his hand on my shoulder and said, "He'll be fine. Thank you, Stephanie."

"Good!" she said, beaming. "One of the crew will come get you when it's time, and she'll bring you all the way up to the entrance. There's a red-light-green-light system set up at the back end of the set, right next to the door you'll use to get on stage. Just wait for that light to turn green, and on you go!"

"And on you go," Dad repeated once she'd left. He squeezed my shoulder. "I know this is not going to be easy for you, Addison."

"Nervous?" Casey asked. She had a long plastic tray in her hand with ovals of color running along it. It reminded me of the cheap paint kits we used in art class, only the colors in hers weren't smeared together into the same dark blackish-green.

"Yeah," I admitted, happy that I'd gotten my vocal cords working. I think it helped that she was looking down at her palette instead of at me. She had a puffy brush, and she was dabbing it into one of the lighter brown colors. I thought she was going to powder my face with it, but from the other side, Vic pressed something cold, wet, and squishy right beneath my black eye. It stung.

"Just a bit of foundation to cover up the bruising," Vic explained. The dusty stuff came after that. I had never put on makeup before, much less blush or eyeliner, but they used it all. When they were done, they swiveled my chair so I could see the mirror. Amazingly, I could barely see any of the black eye. I blinked and opened my mouth wide, then closed it. The makeup was so thick I could actually feel every little part of my face moving. I reached up, worried that it was going to flake off and fall into my lap or something.

"Don't touch it, big guy," Casey warned. "It'll smudge. I know it's weird. Just imagine what it's like to be an actor in a sci-fi movie. You should see some of the makeup they have to wear!"

Vic and Casey started talking about different space movies as they finished up. It was comforting having them chat over me, kind of like I was a statue they were sculpting. My face certainly felt like it was made of clay, and I kept moving my mouth around, watching my reflection in the mirror. Did I always look so old?

It was right about as Casey brought up the newest Marvel movie that a stage manager poked her head in.

"Is Addison ready?" she asked, swiping her headset mic out of the way.

Vic stared closely at my face. She reached up with her pinkie nail and flicked an eyelash off my cheek. Then she nodded.

"Have fun, Addison!" Casey said as she nudged me forward. My dad gave me a double thumbs-up. I took a few deep breaths and tried to swallow. It wasn't easy.

The stage manager led me around the back of the fake kitchen, hopping over wires, dodging other crew members, and finally settling right beneath the red lightbulb. Then she hunched down and crooked her finger to let me know I should join her. Once I squatted next to her, she leaned in, her forehead nearly touching mine. She smelled like coffee.

"All right, kid," she whispered, just like Coach in the last two minutes of a nail-biter. "When that light hits green, here's what you're gonna do: push the door open, step through, then immediately shut it. We don't want the audience or cameras picking up that there isn't a lovely old oak tree, a tire swing, and an aw-shucks-isn't-that-adorable picket fence out here, you get my drift?"

I nodded.

"Good. Once you shut the door, you turn to face the audience. Smile and wave, but don't do it for any longer than three seconds or you look ridiculous. Also, don't count the three seconds out loud; the mic will pick it up if you do. When you're done, stop waving, but keep smiling. Walk around to the right of the couch. That's your right, not the camera's right. Darcy and Rob will be standing. Give Darcy a hug, but make sure to keep your face to the left of hers—that's your left, not Darcy's. If you go in on the right, your chin will brush her mic, and the audience will get an earful of you two snuggling. Darcy will pat your back twice to let you know when to disengage. Once you do, reach over with your right hand to shake with Rob. That's your right, not his. Then you can sit down on the couch. Give the audience another wave, because they'll still be clapping. When they quiet down, Darcy will lead off. Her lines are on the teleprompter. You look at her, not the prompter. After that, it's just keeping your eyes on the person who asked you the last question—let us worry about camera angles and all that. Understood?"

I closed my eyes, trying to imagine it like a play drawn up on Coach's whiteboard. It helped, even though Coach had never told us to hug the other team before. When I thought I had the basics down, I murmured, "Yeah."

She nodded, then reached up to clip something to my collar.

"This is your mic. Gonna attach the pack to your belt. Don't mess with it, or I'll personally track you down and murder you."

My eyes widened.

"Nah, just kidding," she whispered, winking. She fiddled with a few dials, then flipped a switch. Then she pressed a finger to my lips. "But seriously, kid. Don't mess with it."

I reached up to cross my heart, and she gave me a thumbs-up.

"You're live in thirty seconds. Mic will be hot in thirty-five. Welcome to *Mornings with Darcy and Rob*!"

I felt a little bead of sweat roll from my armpit, tickling my rib cage. I should've been going over the stage manager's instructions, but instead I spent the final thirty seconds before my talk-show debut sniffing myself. I had remembered to put on deodorant, at least.

Not a great last thought to be pondering as the light hit green.

I shot up, reaching for the doorknob, but I went in too fast. My fingertips smacked into the knob, and the pain was so bad my eyes nearly crossed. Quickly, I used my other hand to turn the knob, and I kicked the door open with my foot. The roar of applause overwhelmed me—it was much louder than I thought it'd be. It actually hurt my ears. Worse, the lights were right in my face, and instinctively, I lifted my hand to shield my eyes.

What was supposed to be a smile-and-wave turned into a wince-and-block. Several seconds ticked by, and I could hear my brain starting to tear.

But I didn't need to think. I had a game plan.

I stepped around the couch to my right.

Darcy was standing there applauding, all blond hair and green suit and jingly bracelets. I leaned down to hug her.

My left.

When I moved over to shake Rob's hand, he was already waiting with it extended. Then, abruptly, he pulled it back.

"Whoa, there, Michael Jackson!" he said. "Nice glove!"

And just like that, my game plan fell apart.

I kept my hand sticking out there. He was supposed to shake it. *Why wasn't he shaking it?*

A bit of dark blood bloomed in the padding at the tip of my middle finger. I must have hit it even harder than I thought. Rob turned to the audience, chuckled, and pointed at me. "Kid really likes his handshakes! Must've been what he was looking for when he reached out to catch that friend of his!"

The audience erupted in laughter. I pulled my hand back and tried to shove it in my pocket. It wouldn't fit with the glove on, though.

"Just kidding, Addison!" Rob said. "Let's try the other hand!"

He reached down with both hands, grabbed my left, and shook it warmly. He had a closely trimmed beard, a receding hairline, and big shoulders. When he smiled, his nostrils flared, and I could see the hair in there, too. It reminded me to keep staring at him as he talked.

"Have a seat, Mr. Hero!" Rob continued, and he pointed at the couch behind me.

Darcy added, "Yes! Join us! We've been dying to meet the internet's newest sensation and Los Angeles's best catcher since Mike Piazza!"

I stumbled back onto the couch. The seat was harder than I expected, and I bounced a bit as I sat. I tried to keep my eyes on Darcy, but I might as well have been staring right at the spotlight, her hair and jewelry were so shiny. So I dared a glance at the audience.

I couldn't see anything. It was like the world stopped right where the carpet was cut in two. I knew they were out there because I could hear them, but for all I could tell, the world beyond the stage might have been swallowed up into space. It meant I couldn't find my dad, or Stephanie, or Vic, or Casey, or anyone. It felt even scarier than the principal's office.

And this time, I didn't have Devin to help me.

"Well, as many of you know," Darcy exclaimed as she sat down, "Addison Gerhardt is the boy responsible for the high-light play of last Saturday's Clippers game—and he managed to pull it off while being over a hundred yards from the court! Check it out!"

Darcy pointed out into the darkness. I peered. Still

nothing. Rob leaned over and tapped my leg. "We're show-ing your clip for eight seconds. It'll be on the TV screens for the viewers."

I tried to thank him for the explanation, but he looked away and made a little cutting gesture with his hand. Man, eight seconds went by quickly.

"Just amazing, Addison!" Darcy said. "So, I think what everyone is wondering is what led up to that incredible, terrifying moment. Can you tell us a little about that?"

They both smiled broadly, and Darcy rested her elbows on her knees and leaned toward me.

Talk about what happened.

NOPE.

Pretend you're sick and run!

NOPE.

Go find Dad!

NOPE.

Darcy kept smiling. Rob made a little wheel motion with his fingers. Another trickle of sweat danced down the back of my neck.

"I mean," Rob said, "we saw on Twitter that the other kid was a friend of yours. That must have been scary, seeing your friend go over the edge like that, right?"

I tried to say "Uh-huh," but all that came out was a "Huh!" like someone had punched me in the gut. Somebody in the audience coughed. Darcy reached down to get a drink of water from a blue mug next to the flower vase.

"Yeah, I bet it was scary," she said, her smile fading fast. "But not as much as live TV, am I right?"

The audience giggled, and Rob slapped his knee.

"Sure seems like it, Darse! Maybe this one will spark a bit of the old conversation. . . ."

I watched as his eyes flicked toward the teleprompter. I knew I wasn't supposed to look, but I did anyway. It was a see-through screen near the biggest of the cameras, and little ghostlike words scrolled down. He read them off.

"Have you talked to the boy you saved since that evening? What did you say, or what would you say now if you could?"

I barely heard the question. I was praying that the teleprompter would have some words for me, too. But it didn't. His question floated up to the top of the screen, then sat there, nothing but emptiness beneath.

"C'mon, Addison. It's just us here. You can talk to us," Darcy urged.

"And, well, the rest of Los Angeles, and America!" Rob

laughed. Then he turned right to the camera and said quickly, *"Mornings with Darcy and Rob*, now in syndication five days a week. Check local listings for great fun and fascinating interviews, which are apparently just as good on mute as they are with the volume up!"

The audience laughed again, but not as hard as they had before.

Darcy patted my shoulder. "You wouldn't say *anything* to . . . Devin? That's his name, right?"

Frantically, I tried to think. But my throat was closed, and I couldn't come up with any words. There were none on the teleprompter.

There were none in my brain, except maybe NOPE.

But, I realized, there were some in my shoe.

When I leaned down to tug my left loafer off, Darcy flinched. I turned it over and shook it until my note to Devin fell into my lap.

"Here," I managed to mumble. "Hold this."

And then I handed Darcy Warren, the former Miss California and the cohost of Los Angeles's biggest talk show, my brother's old shoe. She took it by the toe, pinching it between her thumb and index finger like something she had just pulled out of a shower drain.

I unfolded the note carefully. A lot of the pencil was smudged, and I had sweat through it a little bit, but it didn't tear. When I had it open, I laid it on my leg and smoothed my palm over it. It crinkled softly under my shaking hands.

Taking a deep breath, just like I had before those fourth-grade book reports, I started to read.

CHAPTER TWENTY-EIGHT

DEAR DEVIN

Dear Devin,

I finally figured out why you punched me in the face.

At first I thought it was because I saved your life, but that wasn't it. For a while, I blamed my freezing, only it wasn't that, either. It wasn't even Twitter, the Velma Curse, that stupid dishwasher, or the Golden State Warriors.

Nope.

It was the Double-Barreled Monkey Bar Backflip of Doom.

We both know I'm not the best at talking. I freeze,

and I choke up, and everything gets tangled. That's why I've always needed you. Remember in kindergarten when I got into the Goldfish? You saved me. You're always saving me, and you've been so good at talking for so long that I never thought there'd be a time when you'd be like me: a time when you'd have no words.

But then your dad had the heart attack, and you didn't have the words. So you talked by doing the Backflip. You were trying to tell me something, over and over, and I didn't get it.

I get it now, though.

It's about being afraid. Like, so afraid that you can't even remember what it was like before you were scared. So you started doing stuff to tell us you were afraid. And your dumb best friend, the guy who should understand being afraid better than anyone, thought you were just trying to get attention, when what you really wanted was support.

Well, I want you to know that I'm sorry. I take it back. You've got my support, and my appearance fee, if you want it. My parents said it's for college, but

I'm going to tell them to give it to you. I wouldn't even be going on the show if it wasn't for you anyway, and if I survive, it's because I'm thinking of you.

Also, I forgive you for punching me. You might not care at this point, but if you're like me, then you've learned something else this week: feeling guilty about hurting your best friend is worse than being afraid. I know that for a fact, and if I can help you not have to feel what I feel, then that might be the very best thing I can do. So I forgive you, and I hope you'll let me help you fight the Curse, because even if I drop your phone, or I freeze, or I mess up, one thing is for sure. I'll always catch you, Devin.

Your best friend,
Addison

CHAPTER TWENTY-NINE

SHOWSTOPPER

When I finished reading, I folded the note up carefully, using the same crease lines that I'd made before. I set it on the couch beside me, and I reached over to grab my shoe from Darcy, who was still holding it up.

"Thanks," I mumbled. She didn't say anything, but her mouth was wide open.

I slipped the note into the loafer, then crammed my foot back in. I stomped on the floor to get my heel in there. Then I put my hands on my knees and pushed myself to a stand. I hugged Darcy again (my left) and shook hands with Rob (his right). Neither of them moved, except when I jiggled Rob's hand. Then I took my mic off, dropped it on the couch, and walked into the darkness.

"Dad," I said, "I'm ready to go now."

I still couldn't see too well, but I felt an arm around my shoulder, and I knew it was him. We walked out past the ladders and the lights, past all the headsets and black shirts. It was awfully quiet behind us. When we were in the parking lot, my dad pulled out his phone and called his buddy.

"Yeah, we're done a little early, Steiner. Do you have a fare, or can you swing up and grab us?"

"Hold that request!" a voice screeched from behind us. It was Stephanie, who was running so hard she nearly skidded right past us.

I wiped the sweat from my forehead, forgetting that there was a ton of makeup on there. My arm came away sticky.

"Addison," Stephanie gasped, trying to catch her breath. "Addison, wait a sec!"

Apologize for ruining their show.

NOPE.

Apologize for embarrassing them on live TV.

NOPE.

Look. We just bombed that show. Like, one hundred megaton, drop-it-in-the-ocean-and-unleash-Godzilla-type bombed.

We sat there sweating like a pig. We took our shoe off and read a note to a kid who wasn't even in the room. We probably bled on their couch, and then we walked straight off their stage way before we were supposed to. You're telling me that after all that, you can't manage a little apology? What could possibly happen that could be worse than what we just did? Apologize!

THAT MAKES SENSE, I GUESS.

"I'm sorry, Stephanie," I whispered.

Wait. That worked?

MAYBE.

"Sorry?" she panted. "Sorry? Addison, can't you hear that?"

She pointed back through the double doors. At first all I could hear were the honks and growls of the traffic outside, but when I concentrated, I could hear something else, like the static on a bad TV channel.

"That's applause, Addison! You asked us why we don't rehearse? *You* are why we don't rehearse. *You* are why live programming is still the best medium in entertainment. Lord, *you* are why people like me have jobs. Will you come back inside? The segment is over; we're on a six-minute commercial break. Darcy and Rob would like to take a picture or two with you, and I'm sure the audience would love a chance at a few autographs."

I looked at my dad, who shrugged. I did, too.

My face was smeared with streaky makeup. My hand was bandaged and bleeding. And they wanted pictures? And autographs?

Being famous was *weird*.

We did go back in, and we did get our pictures taken. I stabbed a pen down at about two dozen notebooks, but I couldn't bring myself to look at who was holding them. Darcy and Rob were thrilled with me, apparently—Stephanie informed them after the second photo that their show was the number one trending topic on Twitter for all of California. They were already trying to get my clip up on YouTube before anyone else could. Rob was brainstorming titles for the video. I think they went with "Kid Catches Friend, But Drops Mic."

Just before the next segment started, and right as Dad's buddy texted to say he was outside, Darcy found me. She gave me another hug—a real one, on the right this time—and said, "Any chance we can get you back onstage to finish the interview, Addison?"

I shook my head so fast my lips jiggled.

She laughed softly, then stepped back. "No pressure. You've given us more than enough. After all, we don't get a lot of real on our show, so it can be a shock when it walks through the door, sits down, and reacquaints us with how messy, uncomfortable, and beautiful it can be. We appreciate the reminder."

I smiled, and Dad shook her hand. Then I took a big, deep, lung-busting breath, and I sighed.

I still had a half day of school ahead of me, after all.

CHAPTER THIRTY

DINNER AT DEVIN'S

It turned out to be a great time to be grounded, since that's pretty much how I was living anyway. The rest of the week was all about hiding in my bedroom, dodging reporters, and declining more shows. We were even getting calls from New York City; *The Tonight Show* offered to fly all of us out there for a day. My mom told them I'd missed too much school already. I thought it was a good excuse, since I didn't think I could survive any more TV time.

On Saturday, I asked her if reading the note on live TV counted as sharing it with Devin.

"Addison," she replied, "I am so very proud of you. Reading your note was incredibly brave, and I felt your sincerity right here in my heart."

"So I'm not grounded anymore?"

"Child, what kind of mother do you think I am? Of course you're still grounded. I don't see Devin Velma with a note pressed into his palm, do I? Fortunately, though, you'll get your chance tonight at our regular dinner at the Velmas' house."

I was shocked; I thought for sure it would have been canceled. Apparently, though, our parents had been scheming about this ever since Devin had first gotten suspended, because they had it all planned out. Mom had even baked brownies.

"When we get there, Addison, you'll say hello to the family, and then march straight up to Devin's room. You knock, and don't stop knocking until he opens that door. Understood?"

"What if he doesn't want to talk?"

"Be persistent, honey," Mom said, "because there's only two ways you're coming down to dinner: with Devin, or with another black eye."

"Mom!" I gasped.

"Shoot for the former, Addison," Mom joked.

"But be ready for the latter," Dad added, and he shadowboxed a bit.

"You two sound like Benji at school," I murmured. "He's in fourth grade."

"Wise fourth grader!" Mom said, and she shooed me out to the taxi.

Mrs. Velma was waiting on the path to their front door as we pulled up, her hands on the handles of Mr. Velma's wheelchair. Both of them waved at us, and when Mrs. Velma stepped inside to put my mom's brownies in the kitchen, Mr. Velma beckoned me into a kneel.

"We watched you on TV, Addison."

"Yes, sir."

"I'm grateful that my son has a friend like you, and not just because you saved his life."

"Is he, um, grateful, too?"

Mr. Velma rolled his eyes and glanced upward. The light was on in Devin's room.

"He is, even if he doesn't know it yet. The Gs have been working on him, and as you know, they can be quite persuasive."

I smiled and nodded, then started up the steps to the house. Mr. Velma caught me by the arm, though.

"One more thing, Addison."

"Yes," my dad added. "And you need to listen, son."

Mr. Velma pressed a hand over his chest. "I told my son after the show, and now I'm telling you. This? My heart?"

My dad put a hand on Mr. Velma's shoulder. "My job, our apartment . . ."

"These are not for you to worry about. They are not your problems."

"I want to hear you say it, Addison," Dad pressed.

I looked down at my new shoes. I wished I had a piece of paper to read from then.

"They're not . . . not our problems," I managed through trembling lips.

"That's right, Addison," Mr. Velma said softly. "It is incredibly gracious of you to offer your appearance fee to us, but you have to know there is no way we're taking it."

"Your insurance, though . . ."

Mr. Velma shook his head.

"We are in a difficult spot, Addison. That's true. But selling our store? Getting a second mortgage? Those are difficulties we are prepared to accept. My son growing up without a father? My son forced to grow up too soon *because* of his father? Those are tragedies, and those I refuse to accept. Your father and I, your mother and Devin's mother, your brother and his sister in college, and all Devin's grandmas—

we work very hard precisely so you and Devin don't have to worry. It brings us joy and comfort knowing that you are still boys. So do *your* jobs, and just be kids for a while longer. Deal?"

My dad nodded, and I exhaled.

"I think we can handle that."

I shook Mr. Velma's hand, and my dad and I helped Mr. Velma into the house.

Inside, I could smell corn, baked beans, and hamburgers on the grill. We found the Gs and Mrs. Velma sitting at the kitchen table, chopping vegetables and putting them on a tray. I said hello, and they patted my cheek or shoulder like everything was normal. Triple-G even offered me the plate of vegetables and dip, because she knew I was always hungry. I eagerly went for the carrots.

Then I screamed.

Triple-G's dentures were right in the middle of the tray, grinning up at me. My hand pulled back so fast that I flung a carrot across the kitchen. It pinged off a pan hanging over the stove.

"That's disgusting, Mama," Double-G said, but she was laughing. So was everyone else.

"Nice one, Triple-G," I added, saluting her.

She winked, and Mrs. Velma mentioned that dinner would be ready soon.

"Addison," my mom said as she picked up a potato peeler, "I think now would be a good time to go find Devin. He's upstairs."

I looked around the table, and the women of the Velma family all smiled at me. Mr. Velma was right. They *were* strong, and knowing that things were all right with them gave me the courage to climb those stairs.

It didn't make my voice any less shaky, though, or my knocking any less clumsy when I reached Devin's room.

"Hey, Devin? It's me, Addison," I said after a few heavy fist thumps on the door.

"It's not locked," I heard.

At least he was talking. That was a good start. Now I just had to . . .

Open the door.

WILL THIS BE AS SCARY AS *MORNINGS WITH DARCY AND ROB*?

Can anything be as scary as Mornings with Darcy and Rob?

FAIR POINT.

When I swung the door open, I saw Devin sitting on his

bed. He had a bunch of Legos piled on the comforter in front of him, and it looked like he maybe hadn't showered in a few days. His hair was sticking out every which way, his face was greasy, and his glasses were on the pillow next to him. It made him seem older somehow. He picked up a gray brick and carefully snapped it into place with the others he had aligned. I recognized what he was building instantly.

"The *Millennium Falcon*," I muttered.

"Remember when we built this four years ago?" he said. He hadn't looked at me yet. Maybe because he didn't want to see the bruise by my eye? I couldn't blame him—it had turned a strange yellow-and-green combination in the last few days.

"Yeah. Right after we saw *Return of the Jedi* for the first time."

"I hate it when Lando flies it. It's not the *Falcon* without Han Solo and Chewbacca."

I dared to sit down on the bed. An avalanche of Legos tumbled against my hip as the mattress sagged. I pushed them back into the pile.

"What made you want to rebuild it?" I asked.

"Dunno. It was something to do while I was grounded. I thought I'd remember how fun these were and get into it."

"Are you? Into it, I mean?"

He looked up then, and he flinched when he saw my face. "Not as much. Not sure why. *Force Awakens*, maybe?"

I crossed myself. "We agreed . . ."

"Not to talk about *Force Awakens*. Yes, I remember. Your eye looks cool."

I reached up to rub at it. "Thanks."

Devin set down the *Millennium Falcon.*

"I'm sorry I punched you," he offered, and he slipped his glasses on. I picked up a few gray pieces and locked them together, a familiar little jolt of accomplishment tickling my fingertips. Reaching over, I stuck them onto the model of the spaceship, right where I remembered them being.

"I wrote you a note," I said after a few moments. Then I reached down to take off my shoe.

"I know. I saw you on TV."

I blushed, putting my foot back down. "I was terrible. It made me kind of hope you couldn't watch TV while you were grounded."

"I can't, but my mom and dad made an exception. They even recorded it and had me watch it twice."

"So," I said, "I guess you know I'm sorry, too."

"Yeah, only you can keep the note. Is it still in your shoe?"

"Yeah. It's a little hard to read; it got all soggy in there."

"Gross."

"Gross," I agreed.

For a couple of minutes, we worked on the *Falcon*, fishing through the clacking pile of Legos and adding pieces whenever we found a good one. It wasn't awkward like I thought it might be, or nerve-racking, or weepy-making. It just *was*, and it felt good, almost like we were back when *The Tonight Show* was a signal that it was past my bedtime, rather than an opportunity to royally embarrass myself.

As I worked on one of the laser cannons, I said, "I bet my letter got you a ton of followers."

Devin smirked. "Doubt it, since I don't have a Twitter account anymore. After my mom talked to yours, that was the first thing to go. Yours is gone, too. Mom stood over my shoulder and made sure I completely nuked them. She said that if I didn't know how to treat my best friend, I sure as hell didn't deserve seventy thousand more."

"Sorry," I murmured.

"She wasn't wrong, Addi."

I nodded. "Trust me, I know. I had, what, two million?"

"Three-point-two by the time I deleted it."

"Okay, so I had three-point-two million followers, and not a single one could help me on that stage. I had to yank a crusty old note out of my shoe and pretend I was talking to you just to get through it."

Devin flicked a piece over to me. I picked it up and put it into place without thinking. It was a perfect fit.

"Your note, by the way. It made me think. You were right. I was afraid. And when I started getting followers . . . well, it felt good. Every time I looked, there were more people. It helped me . . . forget? No. Not forget that my dad was sick. But it was something to do, so that it didn't feel like there was nothing I *could* do, you know?"

I nodded. "I know."

"But they didn't really have my back. Not like you."

"Yup. That's all I really wanted to say."

Devin swept the pile of Legos out of the way and inched next to me.

"Are you cured?"

"Huh?"

"Your freezing. You managed to make it through the entire show. That's, like, the biggest exposure of all. Did it help?"

I shrugged. "It was just as hard to climb those steps to talk to you. I don't think *cured* is how it works."

"But you made progress?"

"A little, maybe? I'm not sure. Helps when you're there, though."

Devin nodded and picked up a little yellow Lego guy. Double-G called from downstairs that dinner was ready, and my stomach reminded me that it didn't like being ignored for long. I hopped up.

"You coming?"

"I dunno . . ." He paused, tugging off the Lego guy's legs, then reattaching them backward. "Your mom and dad . . . this is the first time they're going to see me since I punched their kid in the face. Are they mad?"

I smiled. "Doubt it. But I know one way to find out for sure."

Devin adjusted his glasses.

"How?"

I swung his door open wide and stepped into the hallway.

"Follow me."

ACKNOWLEDGMENTS

In a perfect world, we'd pack arenas like the Staples Center for book launches and children's literature events. And when it came time to show the MVPs on the jumbotron, they'd display pictures of editors like Liz Szabla. Without her, Addison doesn't find his inner voice, Devin misses his motivation, and I don't go back for that last essential look. Surrounding Liz in the photo would be the team at Feiwel and Friends, who make dreams come true—Jean, Rich, Lauren, Anna, Allison, Mary, Molly, Morgan, and everyone who supports them.

Coach of the year goes to Rebecca Stead, of course. She always seems to know the right play, her guidance is expert, and her knowledge of craft is unmatched. I'm absurdly lucky to learn from her.

Thanks, too, to all my second readers, who were vital in helping make sure this book was ready to take the court in the first place: Adam Solomon, Jen Shaw, Anna Priemaza, Roberto Garza, Caroline Huber, Caitlin Simon, Greg Huber, Jennifer Friedman, Jim Adams, Ruthann and Theodore Gill, and Donald and Donna Burt.

Oh, and Elizabeth, Lauriann, and Lyra? You guys are the best fans ever.

JAKE BURT

What did you want to be when you grew up?
I wanted to start as point guard for the Golden State Warriors. Unfortunately, I think I'm somewhere around fourteen millionth on the depth chart.

When did you realize you wanted to be a writer?
Eighth grade. That's the first time I can remember having a story stuck in my head that I couldn't stop thinking about. Writing it down was the only way to give my brain a break. Of course, once I indulged that one story, dozens more figured they could get the same treatment, and I was hooked.

What's your most embarrassing childhood memory?
It has to be the only time I ever cheated on anything. In first grade, we had a worksheet that asked us to color eggs in three different colors. Then we had to cut them out and paste them to another sheet that had the corresponding names of the colors. I stank at color words, for some reason. I pasted mine on there and got every single one wrong. When I went to turn it in, I saw my friend Chris's paper. He rocked at colors. Seeing that his eggs were in different positions than mine, I decided I was going to fix mine to match his. Simple enough, right? Just peel mine off while the paste was still

wet, then move them to match Chris's eggs. Yeah, I see that now. Back then? My genius self decided the best way to handle things was to peel Chris's eggs off his paper and stick them on mine, and move my eggs to his paper. In doing so, I mutilated both papers, got caught, and had to apologize to Chris and the teacher in front of the whole class. Then I had to take my ripped-up, paste-saturated guilt rag home in a plastic bag to show my parents while I explained myself.

What's your favorite childhood memory?
Playing made-up games in our backyard with my brothers and all the neighborhood kids. I'm convinced it was a critical part of my creative development. Whether it was imagining that we were fighting in Thunderdome after the third *Mad Max* movie came out, or slamming half-deflated soccer balls into aluminum trash cans in homage to *American Gladiator*, we managed to amuse the heck out of ourselves.

As a young person, who did you look up to most?
I looked up to my dad. Still do.

What was your favorite thing about school?
Since we moved around a little when I was a kid, it took me a while to settle in at school. Once I did, though, my friendships were my favorite part. 'Round about eighth grade, I found where I belonged, and with whom. It made all the difference.

What were your hobbies as a kid? What are your hobbies now?
I obsessed about basketball, played board games, and read books. Now? Yeah, it's pretty much the same thing, though I've diversified to Ultimate Frisbee and banjo playing, too.

Did you play sports as a kid?
I played basketball daily, though never for the school team. I was more of a YMCA gym rat. We had a hoop in our backyard, too, and we'd get some vicious games going back there.

What was your first job, and what was your worst job?
My first job was working as a horticulturist at a graveyard. I'd love to say that's a euphemism for grave digger, but it really just meant I pulled poison ivy off the fences and dealt with the underground hornets' nests. My worst job was operating a hydraulic press at a gasket factory. It was the monotony that got to me. I couldn't handle doing the same thing, over and over, for eight hours a day. I learned that quickly. That's why I love teaching and writing.

What book is on your nightstand now?
Slayer by Kiersten White. It's a jump from all the middle grade fiction I read, but I'm a huge *Buffy the Vampire Slayer* fan, so I had to check it out.

How did you celebrate publishing *The Right Hook of Devin Velma*?
Since it's my second novel, I sort of knew what was coming on launch day. It was actually more laid-back than you might think; the party and book tour came afterward. We went out to dinner all quietlike. The launch party itself, though, was a lot of fun. I filled a huge crystal bowl with Goldfish crackers, and I got an audience of over a hundred people to play a game of "Are You a Devin or an Addison."

Where do you write your books?
I do the bulk of my writing in my office, spinning on my exercise desk. *Greetings from Witness Protection!* was written on

a makeshift one—I tore apart an old exercise bike until it was just the seat and the pedals. Then I put two tables on either side, stacked chairs on top of that, then laid another table leaf across that. Once I slid the exercise bike under there, I could ride it while typing on my laptop. It was dangerous and noisy, though, so to reward myself for publishing the book, I bought a swanky new desk-bike. That's where I wrote *Devin*.

What sparked your imagination for *The Right Hook of Devin Velma*?

It was mostly my anxiety over using social media. As a published author, it's important to have ways that my readers can access me. That means keeping up a website, getting on Twitter, and responding to fans' emails as promptly as possible. I've never considered myself savvy at any facet of maintaining a public persona, so when it came time for me to do so, I found it quite difficult. Much of that difficulty went into Addison; his reluctance to put himself out there (or to bask in it once he is famous) closely mirrors my own angsty relationship with self-promotion.

What challenges do you face in the writing process, and how do you overcome them?

My single greatest challenge is time. Since I teach fifth grade, I have to carve out spaces for my writing to inhabit, and that can get tricky during the school year, especially since I need at least a solid two-hour block to be productive. Summer is my writing haven.

What is your favorite word?

I've always been drawn to the names of gemstones. They're pretty to say (*emerald, jacinth, tourmaline, lapis lazuli*), evoke colors, and feel valuable. My favorite of them all is *sapphire*.

If you could live in any fictional world, what would it be?
Lyra's dimension, so I could meet my daemon. (Google it, kids. Then read the books.)

Who is your favorite fictional character?
Oh, man . . . Bilbo? Schmendrick? Sir Gareth of Orkney? Snape? I think I'm going to have to go with Lyra again. I named my cat after her. Almost named my daughter after her, too, but my wife wouldn't let me (she vetoed Bilbo, too . . .).

What was your favorite book when you were a kid? Do you have a favorite book now?
When I was a kid, it was *The Hobbit.* Now, it's *The Hobbit.*

If you could travel in time, where would you go and what would you do?
I'd love to answer this altruistically, but the truth is I'd probably go back in time and give my younger self a bunch of advice . . . and stock tips. Yeah, I know, the continuity stream and the butterfly effect and all that stuff. Still, though . . . ten-year-old Jake running around with a portfolio of Amazon and Google stock? Pretty hard to turn that down.

What's the best advice you have ever received about writing?
The best advice I ever received about writing is to receive advice about writing. I know that sounds weird, but it's true—being willing to find second readers, to seek out critique and respond to it in a healthy way, is absolutely vital. If you want to improve, you have to engage with and respond to your audience at key points during the process.

What advice do you wish someone had given you when you were younger?

See above, re: the older me going back in time to harass younger me. It'd have been great to have someone there to point at things and say, "See that thing you're about to stress out over? It doesn't matter. That other thing? It doesn't matter either. But her? She matters. Be nice to her. Him? He could use some support right now." Lord, I could have saved a bunch of energy that way, but I suppose that's, quite literally, life.

Do you ever get writer's block? What do you do to get back on track?

I don't, actually (knocks furiously on wood). That's not because it all comes breathtakingly easy to me, though. It's because I outline so thoroughly before I write that once I do, it's basically just sculpting around a skeleton already fused in place. And I don't outline something unless I'm sure I want to write it.

What do you want readers to remember about your books?

I'd be humbled beyond belief if they remembered my characters. If, in conversations with friends over cookies or coffee or crumpets, they said, "Hey, you know who else was a strong female protagonist? Nicki, in that one dude's book," or "Remember that Addison kid? I feel kind of like him right now." I'd also enjoy it if they recalled my books as being tolerable and, at times, mildly amusing. Anything more than that is just icing on the cake.

What would you do if you ever stopped writing?

Probably go mad. Or drive my wife and daughter mad. I write because there are stories I feel like I have to tell, and if

I couldn't put them on paper, I'd have to blah-blah-blah them at my family. I'm sure they'd appreciate that . . .

If you were a superhero, what would your superpower be?

I've actually given a ridiculous amount of thought to this. The answer is telekinesis; that is, the ability to manipulate and move objects with the power of my mind. It wouldn't give me headaches or nosebleeds either. I'd just do it. I could lift cars and reorganize rooms and pick myself up to make myself fly, sure, but I could also use it to vibrate molecules so rapidly that things caught on fire, or slow the movement of molecules down until something froze. There are so many things you can do with telekinesis that it's like twelve powers in one.

Do you have any strange or funny habits? Did you when you were a kid?

Three-fourths of everything I do is born out of strange or funny habits; the other fourth is stuff I do in support of my strange or funny habits. One that I had as a kid, and that I've kept into adulthood, is a pathological fear of making two trips while carrying things. Groceries from the car to the house? ONE TRIP. Cereal from the kitchen to the table? ONE TRIP. Gear from the van to the campsite? ONE TRIP. If I can't manage it in a single haul, then it ain't gettin' managed.

What do you consider to be your greatest accomplishment?

My greatest accomplishment is my family. It is the one of which I'm the most proud, the one that brings me my greatest joy, and the one upon which I continue to work the hardest.

What was your favorite scene to write in *The Right Hook of Devin Velma*? What was the most challenging?

My favorite scene is Devin and Addison in Ms. Carrillo's office. It's a quieter scene, sure, but it's where we really see Addison's social anxiety for the first time, and it also features a lot of those weird little details that I think make scenes memorable. In this case, those details include a turtle named Fanny. The most challenging part to write was Addison's letter to Devin. I wanted to make it deeply emotional without getting too prosaic—Addison isn't prone to waxing eloquent, even though his author frequently is. So I started flowery, then pared it back. I still think I could've tuned it a little better, but that's the classic writer's curse.

Did you have to do any special research to write this book?

I've dealt with social anxiety before, but I don't have social anxiety disorder. As a result, the vast majority of my research went into getting the portrayal of it as close to resonant as possible. Note that I didn't say, "as close to correct"—that's because one of the first things I learned is that everyone who grapples with social anxiety disorder does so differently. It manifests in different ways, it has different triggers, and strategies to cope with episodes work differently for each person. Addison's social anxiety is unique to him, and my hope is that his experiences will ring true even if they don't precisely mirror anyone else's.

What would your readers be most surprised to learn about you?

People are generally surprised to hear that I lived in China for a year. What's really surprising, though, is that while I was there, I starred in a commercial for rabbit meat. Some-where out there is a video of me speaking horrible Mandarin and demanding a plateful of cooked rabbit (*tu rou*) from a poor waiter who, misunderstanding my intentional butcher-ing of his language, brings me a platter of potatoes (*tu dou*) instead.

When the class bully finally finds
somebody else to pick on, Bell Kirby must face
an impossible choice. Stand up to Parker—

Or join him.

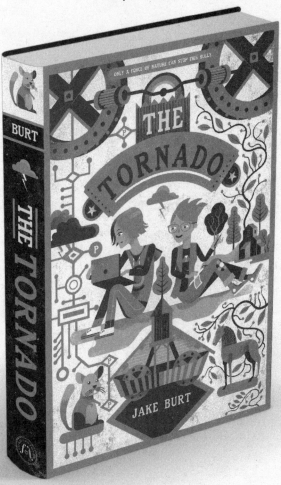

Keep reading for an excerpt.

CHAPTER ONE

B ell Kirby was *supposed* to be drawing a map of Central America. If any of his classmates had bothered to look, they'd have seen him hunched over his desk, scribbling furiously with a black pen. They'd never guess the curves weren't the borders of Honduras or Guatemala, or the straight lines weren't longitude, or that it wasn't even his social studies notebook hidden in the halo of his arms.

And that was just fine with Bell.

He needed all of silent work time to sketch and resketch those strange puzzle pieces his dad had sent. Was one of them a crown? A spinning top? A faucet? He paused, cracking his knuckles and rubbing his ink-stained palms together. All he had to do was concentrate a bit longer, and he was sure he'd have it. Not even Parker Hellickson could distract him—Bell was that zeroed in.

But then Daelynn Gower touched down in his classroom like a tornado.

The door burst open, and a backpack slid across the floor, spewing its contents everywhere: colored pencils, pink erasers, unicorn folders, a purple glasses case, and three mandarin oranges. A pair of green-handled lefty scissors spun dangerously close to Bell's foot, forcing him to lift his legs before his sneaker got skewered.

Just behind the backpack rushed a girl.

"I am *so* sorry! I forgot to re-zip after I got my glasses out, and I didn't know the door was going to open like that! I'll clean it up! Here!" the girl said as she scampered around. She chased an orange all the way up to Mrs. Vicker's desk, then veered toward Bell, leaning down to pick up her scissors. Blushing, he lunged over his notebook to hide what he had drawn . . .

And found himself staring into a rainbow.

The girl's hair was cut short, like a candy-coated cap, and it was dyed turquoise and yellow and magenta. Her glasses, as thick as the ones Bell used to wear before he got contacts, had blocky red rims. When she looked up at Bell, he stifled a gasp.

Her eyes were two different colors, too. The left was a regular shade of eyeball-blue. The right was startlingly green.

She smiled sheepishly at him, revealing two lines of braces, each one featuring a multicolored rubber band. Bell shifted silently in his seat. Inside, he was screaming at the girl to go away. Every second she was near him was a moment that Parker Hellickson was watching, too.

Clenching his teeth, Bell scooted her scissors forward with his toe until she found them and hurried back to the front of the classroom. He only exhaled once he saw that Parker's eyes were narrowed at the new arrival. Still, Bell curled up as small as he could at his desk, just in case, and he pulled a few locks of his shaggy blond hair down like a curtain for good measure.

"Class," Mrs. Vicker muttered after looking skyward and shaking her head. "This is the new student I was telling you about. She'll introduce herself in a moment. Can we remember who *we* are by helping her pick up the things she's dropped?"

A few kids closest to the front slid from their desks, scrounging on the floor for erasers and colored pencils. The girl opened her hands, but she couldn't hold everything, and a couple of erasers escaped to bounce underneath the nearby bookshelf.

"Thank you, Adrienne, Chris, and Zayne. And welcome . . ." Mrs. Vicker paused, checking a piece of paper on her desk. "Die-lynn?"

"It's 'Day,'" the girl replied, pushing up her glasses. "But that's okay. I get all kinds of different things. You can call me 'Dye' if you want. I guess I've got the hair for it."

Bell chuckled briefly, though he bit his lower lip and looked down at the floor when he saw that nobody else was laughing.

"And where was your old school, Daelynn?" Mrs. Vicker asked, hitting the "Day" particularly hard.

"There wasn't one," Daelynn said. "I did homeschooling."

Bell felt every muscle in his neck and back tense at once. He had to force himself to keep breathing. Daelynn rubbed nervously at the logo on the sleeve of her jacket. It looked to Bell like a deer, or maybe a moose. Underneath the jacket, she wore a T-shirt with several anime characters drawn across the front. Her pants were covered in patches, and the one on her left knee seemed to be a flower of some sort. The right knee patch was another of the moose things, just as colorful and shocking as her eyes.

Is this how homeschooled kids dress? he thought.

At least her bright red sneakers looked kind of normal.

Mrs. Vicker cleared her throat. "And where was home?"

"Portland, Oregon."

Bell's teacher nodded appreciatively. "Portland! That's a long way from Cincinnati!"

"Yes, ma'am," Daelynn replied, "and we drove."

"Well, welcome to Village Green Elementary, home of the Pioneers!"

Daelynn smiled, and Mrs. Vicker led her through a few more questions. Bell contemplated opening his notebook again—normally, he'd have spent the entire class with his head hovering a few inches from its pages, pretending to take notes while he drew. This Daelynn, though, was hard to ignore. And it wasn't just the colors, or her breathless entrance, or the homeschooling, or her laugh, which ended just like the last flutters of air squeaking out of a balloon.

She was a new variable in his system, kind of like when they moved the snack table inside for morning recess. It jammed everyone up at the same double doors, especially on chocolate-chip granola bar days. It took Bell three weeks to redesign his route outside, and he'd been tripped and teased and had his granola bar stolen a half dozen times as he tried to figure it out. That had been a bad time.

And, based on the scene Daelynn had made when she came in, this had the potential to be much, much worse.